ALICE JONES
THE GHOST LIGHT

SARAH RUBIN

Chicken House

2 Palmer Street, Frome, Somerset BA11 1DS
chickenhousebooks.com

Text © Sarah Rubin 2017
First published in Great Britain in 2017
Chicken House
2 Palmer Street
Frome, Somerset BA11 1DS
United Kingdom
www.chickenhousebooks.com

Cover and interior design and illustration by Helen Crawford-White
Typeset by Dorchester Typesetting Group Ltd
Printed and bound in by CPI Group (UK) Ltd,
Croydon, CR0 4YY
The paper used in this Chicken House book is made from wood grown
in sustainable forests.

1 3 5 7 9 10 8 6 4 2

British Library Cataloguing in Publication data available.

ISBN 978-1-910002-87-2
eISBN 978-1-911077-21-3

*For Mark Puglisi, Dan Mills, Frank Bachman
and Casey Rush – four fabulous directors
who inspired my love of theatre.*

ALSO BY SARAH RUBIN

Dreamer Ballerina
Alice Jones: The Impossible Clue

CHAPTER 1

'I can't believe this is really happening. I'm going to meet Matthew Strange,' Kevin said for the tenth time in as many minutes.

'Yep,' I said, again.

We were sitting in the empty auditorium of the Beryl Theatre watching rehearsals for *The Curse of the Casterfields*. My twin sister Della stood onstage in an old-fashioned maid's uniform helping her co-star Vivian pretend to get dressed for a ball. Della and my mom had both come up to Philly from New York to put on the play and save the Beryl, and now that it was February break they'd roped me into helping too.

'How can you not be more excited? Matthew Strange is in a show with your sister. *The* Matthew Strange. Agent Zero. Jordan Severe. He's only the best action star ever.

And we get to meet him.' Kevin's voice rose to an excited squeak.

'I thought you said you were going to be cool?'

'I'm cool,' Kevin said quickly.

I turned and stared at him with both my eyebrows raised.

He flashed me his most angelic smile. 'I'm the coolest person you know.'

I snorted and started to reply, but the show's director turned in his seat and glared at me, as if I'd been the one making all the noise. Frank Vallance wore his scowl the way he wore his scarf, with flair. I glanced at Kevin but he was doing his best impression of cherubic innocence. There was no point blaming anything on him.

I shrank down in my seat and closed my mouth. Frank held the glare for a minute, making sure I'd learnt my lesson. Then he gave a satisfied nod and turned back to watching the rehearsal.

'You always get me in trouble,' I whispered.

'Shhh,' Kevin said, halo still firmly in place. 'I'm trying to watch the show.'

The set reminded me of an old-style doll's house, the kind where the front swung open revealing a cross section of the house inside. Each 'room' was separated by a thin partition of wood and some clever lighting. Downstairs, a large entry hall and study. Upstairs, a bedroom and balcony. A staircase painted to look like mahogany connected the two levels.

'No,' Vivian Rollins – the show's leading lady – enunciated, holding up her hand as Della offered her a string of pearls. 'Tonight I will wear diamonds.'

Della's eyes went wide as she played her part. 'Diamonds? But, my lady, what of the curse?'

Vivian sniffed and tossed her hair. 'I am the daughter of Lord Casterfield. I will not be cowed by such foolishness.'

I rolled my eyes. *The Curse* was over-dramatic even by theatre standards.

Della gave a small curtsy and took the pearls to a safe that stood next to the bed like a night table. She mimed turning a dial and pulled the door open. It stuck slightly, but Della didn't let it show on her face. My sister is a total pro. Then she put the pearls inside and pulled out a large diamond necklace.

'Check out that rock.' Kevin half whistled at the sight of it. 'How much do you think that would be worth?'

'It isn't real,' I said.

'But what if it was?'

Frank glared at us again and I snapped my mouth shut.

Della fastened the necklace around Vivian's neck, careful not to block the audience's view.

Then there was silence. A long, awkward silence.

'That was your cue, Matthew,' Frank said, rubbing the bridge of his nose.

The upstage left door popped open and Matthew

Strange stuck his head through the gap. 'Sorry, sorry. Was I late?'

'Matthew, are you sure you don't want someone backstage to cue you in? Pete would be more than happy to—'

'No, no. I'm just a cast member like everyone else. I don't need any special treatment.' Matthew flashed his trademark smile, so white it was almost blinding. 'Just one more take. I'll get it.'

Della and Vivian traded concerned looks and Frank made a face like he'd swallowed a lemon. I wondered if Matthew Strange realized he wouldn't get any do-overs on opening night. Kevin just sat there, grinning.

'All right,' said Frank wearily. 'Let's take it again from the pearls.'

Matthew waved happily at Frank and then caught sight of me in the audience. 'Annie!' he called. 'Be a dear and get me an apple water. I'm parched.'

He didn't wait for a response, just ducked through the door and shut it behind him. I sank a little lower in my seat.

The actors went back to their places, and played the scene again. Della offered the pearls and Vivian demanded the diamonds instead. This time, Matthew made his cue, coming in through the front door of the set as Della did her bit with the safe. Or she tried to, but the door was sticking again. Frank scribbled a note, probably a reminder to get Pete – the Beryl's stage manager – to oil the door.

'Woah, Numbers.' Kevin stared at me, his eyes wide. 'Matthew Strange just *spoke* to you.'

'Did he?' I asked. The last time I checked my name was Alice, not Annie.

'Well, aren't you going to get him his drink?'

I snorted. If Matthew Strange thought I was there to be his personal assistant, he had another thing coming. Besides, if I got the water now, it would be warm by the time they stopped rehearsing. Matthew Strange preferred his apple water chilled.

'What's apple water, anyway?'

I turned to tell Kevin to keep quiet, and that's when Della screamed.

'Look out!'

It wasn't the scream so much as my sister breaking character that made my blood run cold. She'd only do that for a life-or-death emergency.

Matthew Strange dived to the side like a hero in one of his action movies. Time slowed and I watched open-mouthed as the fake wooden safe came loose, tipping over the edge of the set and hurtling down.

The safe missed the movie star's head by centimetres and slammed into his shoulder, driving him into the floor with a sickening thud. Della stood on the edge of the set above him, her face completely bloodless, her hand raised as if she was still holding on to the safe's door.

'Come on,' I said to Kevin, as I jumped over the seat in front of me and ran around the edge of the orchestra pit. Using my hand as a lever, I swung myself on to the stage, and then hauled Kevin up after me. Frank was just a few steps behind us and I helped him up too.

'Matthew! Matthew!' Vivian wailed above us.

Pearls littered the stage and I almost slipped trying to get to where Matthew lay in a heap on the floor. I skidded and came to a stop by his head, my heart thudding with relief when I saw he was still breathing.

Up close Matthew Strange was just as handsome as he looked onscreen. It was eerie, like he was too perfect to be real. As I watched, though, an unhealthy greyness dulled his dark skin. That must have been the pain. His right arm bent out from his shoulder at an angle that made my stomach turn.

Kevin knelt beside Matthew Strange, his star-struck expression replaced with one of calm assessment. Matthew's eyes flashed open and he tried to sit up, yelping with pain.

'My face,' he cried. 'Is my face OK?'

Kevin pushed him back gently.

'What do you think you're doing?' Frank snapped.

'It's OK,' I said. 'His mom's an ER nurse. He knows what he's doing.'

Frank glared at me again, but there wasn't much force to it. 'Fine. Don't let him move. I'll go call 911. And Linda.'

Frank shuddered. I didn't blame him. Linda Beharry was the president of the Save the Beryl campaign. She would *not* be happy if Matthew Strange was seriously injured. He was the show's biggest draw.

'This is just perfect,' Frank groaned as he strode offstage. 'Losing an actor during tech week. As if things weren't bad enough already.'

On the level above us, Vivian was still wailing like a banshee, her screams getting louder the longer no one asked her what was wrong. She hadn't been anywhere near the safe, though, so I wasn't worried about her. Della, on the other hand, had.

'You got this?' I asked Kevin.

He looked up at me and nodded once. He was already pulling off his flannel shirt to make a sling for Matthew's injured arm. Matthew didn't move, just lay there gingerly exploring his face with his uninjured hand, searching for any injury to his striking good looks.

I took the steps two at a time. They were more rickety than they looked. Pete's paint job added depth and shadow and made them look solid from the audience, but they were really just flimsy plywood slats that bounced slightly underfoot.

'Della,' I said once I got to the top. 'You OK?'

That was the last straw for Vivian. She screamed one more time, and then fainted, coincidentally landing across the bed. I ignored her.

'Della?' I asked again, but my sister wasn't listening. She just stood there staring over the edge at Matthew. Her mouth opened in a perfect O.

'Is he . . .?' She didn't finish the question, just let the words fade out.

I rolled my eyes. 'No, he's not dead. But I think he hurt his arm. Go find Jarvis.' The Beryl caretaker was creepy, but he was in charge of fire drills and first aid. 'Frank is calling an ambulance, but I don't know how long they'll take to get here.'

Della nodded, shaking off the role of horrified witness and transforming into the plucky heroine who saves the day. She pelted down the stairs, exiting stage right.

Vivian lay motionless across the bed, her black hair spread out around her like it had been arranged by an artist. I saw her eyes flutter open and then close again. Typical. Vivian needed more of an audience than just me before her dramatic recovery. Her eyes flickered again and I turned my back. She could wait all day as far as I was concerned.

I walked carefully to the edge of the set. It wasn't that high up, but I still shuddered slightly when I looked over the edge. I'm not good with heights. Below me, Kevin was busy immobilizing Matthew's arm.

I knelt down and examined the empty space beside the bed, where the safe had been before it fell. It didn't make sense. The safe should have been bolted to the floor. It shouldn't have fallen even if Della was *trying* to push it over.

Deep, square-edged grooves cut into the plywood floor. I traced their outline with my finger. Someone had prised the safe loose with a crowbar. But why?

The door between the theatre and the lobby banged open and I looked up with a start. Frank was back, and the rest of the small cast and crew followed close behind him, their faces all creased with worry. I took a slow breath and tried not to shiver as a cold chill crawled down my spine.

The real question wasn't 'why?' It was 'who?'

CHAPTER

2

'But did you see the way he dodged it?' Kevin said as we biked down 6th Street.

'I guess all that stunt training came in handy,' I puffed. My breath steamed out into the frosty night and my legs burnt from pedalling through the slush-lined streets.

Kevin grinned. 'He's so cool.'

More like lucky, I thought. The paramedics said Matthew Strange would be fine, he'd need to wear a sling for a few days, but he'd be OK in time for the show. His face would be fine too. But if the safe had hit his head it would have been a very different story. I shivered, remembering the gouge marks on the plywood platform. Why had someone prised the safe loose?

'Are you worried about Della?' Kevin asked when I didn't

reply. Mom had insisted on taking her to be checked at the hospital along with Matthew and Vivian.

I shook my head. 'No, my mom's the worrier.'

Kevin and I turned on to Passfield Avenue and pulled up outside the house I shared with my dad. It was a two-bedroom, brick front with three steps leading up to the front door and wrought-iron bars on the windows. Normally when Della was in town it got pretty crowded, but this time she and Mom were staying in a hotel.

Kevin fell in behind me as I pushed my bike up the stairs and unlocked the front door.

'Dad?' I tossed my backpack on to the brown corduroy couch and shrugged off my coat. The kitchen was empty, and there was nothing on the stove.

The ground floor of our house was one large room. Kitchen to my right and living room to my left. Dad's office was off the back of the living room. I stuck my head through the door, but he wasn't there either.

'Dad?' I called again.

'Wait there,' Dad called back from upstairs. There was a pause and then his bedroom door opened and shut and Dad came waltzing down the stairs. 'Well, what do you think?' he asked from the bottom of the steps. 'Do I look like James Bond, or do I look like James Bond?'

He was wearing a tuxedo, complete with bow tie. The Moleskine notebook he usually kept tucked in his back pocket poked out from the top of his cummerbund. I had to admit, he didn't look bad. In fact, if I thought my dad was capable of standing still for more than three seconds at a time he might have a chance of pulling off suave. Then he started to fidget, and the illusion cracked. James Bond never fidgeted.

'Look, there's even a camera in the bow tie! Neat, huh?'

'Looking good, Mr Jones,' Kevin said.

'Kevin! How nice to see you. Are you staying for dinner? I ordered takeaway.' He looked behind us. 'Where's Della?'

I winced. We'd been swapping dinners between Mom and Dad since Della got to town. Tonight was supposed to be Dad's turn. Part of me was looking forward to when this show was over and things would go back to normal. My stomach twisted and I felt rotten for thinking it, but it was the truth. Things were just easier when Mom and Dad were in different states.

'There was an accident at the theatre,' I said, and then added quickly, 'Della's fine, but Mom insisted on taking her to the hospital.'

'What happened?' Dad asked, his voice full of concern.

'Part of the set fell. It hit Matthew Strange, but he's OK. And Della wasn't hurt at all.'

'Seriously, Mr Jones,' Kevin added as he took off his coat and made himself at home. 'Della was barely accident adjacent.'

'Ah, I see,' Dad said. He knew what Mom was like, but

he still looked disappointed. 'I'll give her a call to check in later.'

Back when I was eight and my mom and dad had split up, Mom had moved to New York City with Della and I'd stayed in Philly with Dad. We saw each other most holidays, but I knew Dad wished he could see Della more. Mom probably felt the same way about me.

'So, what's with the penguin suit?' I asked, trying to change the subject.

An unmistakable spark lit up Dad's entire face. Story Fever. Dad's a crime reporter for the *Philadelphia Daily News*. The only thing he likes more than nosing out a good story is telling the world all about it.

'What's the case?'

'Nothing specific yet. I'm trying to get an interview with the elusive Rex Cragthorne.'

I grimaced.

The doorbell rang and Dad smoothed back his hair and did his best to look suave as he answered it. The delivery guy did a quick double take as he handed Dad a bag from Golden Empress. The smell of spring rolls and hot and sour soup made my stomach growl.

'Who's Rex Cragthorne?' Kevin asked while Dad paid for the food.

'He owns Kingdom Cinemas,' I said. Cragthorne owned a lot of other media companies too, but that was the one he was famous for. He was also famous for his shady business deals, though he'd never actually been caught doing anything illegal. I bet Dad was trying to change that.

Dad turned round, arms full, and elbowed the door shut. 'He's notoriously private. He almost never leaves his New York penthouse. And he *never* talks to the press. But thanks to Linda Beharry and my ex-wife, he's here all week.'

Kevin gave me a blank look.

'He's trying to buy the Beryl so he can tear it down and build a multiplex instead,' I explained. 'He's the whole reason Linda started the Save the Beryl campaign.'

'Ooooh,' Kevin said, snapping his fingers. 'He's the "ill-faced, worse-bodied crook" Linda and Frank keep moaning about.'

'That's the one.'

Dad started unpacking the takeaway bags while I grabbed a stack of plates from the kitchen and laid them out on the counter. I tossed Dad an apron from the hook next to the refrigerator. Dad plus chopsticks plus a rental tux was an equation for disaster.

'I thought they were trying to save the Beryl because of some old fire,' Kevin said, pulling up a stool.

I waved my hand in the air, the universal sign for 'it's complicated'.

Dad paused mid-scoop. 'The 1927 fire is what wrecked the inside of the building. People have been talking about restoring the Beryl for years. But it wasn't until Rex

Cragthorne tried to buy it from the city that they had a deadline. In a way, he's the reason the Save the Beryl campaign finally came together and got something done.'

'Don't let Mom hear you say that,' I said, and wished I hadn't. Dad would never do that, and telling him not to felt way too close to getting between them. I took a bite and swallowed too soon, then took a drink to force the lump of food down. I pointed at Dad's suit with my chopsticks. 'So how does the tuxedo help you interview his royal evilness?'

Dad grinned at me. 'Well,' he said, leaning across the table, 'you know how all the museums and galleries hold fundraisers around Valentine's Day?'

I nodded – that had been one of the ideas Mom and Linda had had for raising money for the Beryl, before they decided putting on a show would be more appropriate.

'One of my sources told me which events Cragthorne is attending while he's in town. These are pretty fancy affairs, too. Everyone who's anyone in Philly will be there. I'm going to the Liberty Ball tonight, and the tickets cost a thousand dollars a plate.'

Kevin made a choking sound. I whistled, then waited to see if he needed me to smack him on the back.

Kevin took a sip of water and cleared his throat. 'Seriously?' he asked, his eyes streaming. 'What are they serving? Lobsters stuffed with gold?'

I handed Kevin a napkin. 'It's one thousand dollars for

the ticket, not the food. Most of the money goes to the museum. That's why it's called a fundraiser.'

'Still sounds crazy to me. Who has that kind of money?'

My stomach lurched. 'Wait. Dad. You didn't buy a ticket, did you?'

I didn't think the paper would let him put a thousand-dollar fundraiser ticket on his expense account. And I knew *we* didn't have that kind of money.

'Of course not,' Dad said. 'I'm going undercover.' He draped his napkin over one arm and held out the tray of spring rolls with the other, bending twenty degrees at the waist in a stiff little bow.

I could feel my eyebrows creeping up my forehead. 'You're going undercover as a waiter?'

'Of course. If I can get close to Cragthorne, it could be the scoop of the century!' He took a look at the clock. It was almost six. His eyes popped and he ate the rest of the food on his plate in three giant bites. It was a good thing I'd given him the apron. 'I gotta run, sweetie. Catering needs to be there before the party starts. You kids have fun.'

And with that he pulled off his apron, grabbed his coat and flew out the door.

'Your dad is crazy,' Kevin said around a mouthful of mushu pork.

Outside on the street, I heard Dad's ancient Plymouth station wagon screech into traffic and three different horns protesting forcefully. Dad's driving philosophy is *they have brakes.*

I shrugged. My dad did go a little overboard sometimes, but I wouldn't call him crazy. He was just passionate about his job.

We finished eating and Kevin helped me wash the dishes, drying each plate as I handed it to him and moaning that we didn't own a dishwasher.

'It's just me and my dad. We don't have enough plates to fill a dishwasher.'

Kevin shook his head and put away the last plate. 'You are living in the Stone Age.'

I handed him the last plate with a smile.

I'd just put two mugs of milk in the microwave to make hot chocolate, when the front door opened. I looked up, expecting to see Dad, but instead my sister stood scowling in the doorway.

'Della, are you all right?' I asked. 'Where's Mom?'

'She had to take Irinke her dress for the Liberty Ball. She's picking me up on her way back to the hotel,' Della said as she swept into the room, loosening her gloves one finger at a time.

I rolled my eyes. Irinke Barscay was the Beryl's 'angel'. That meant she had a lot of money and enjoyed spending it on theatre productions. It also meant everyone at the Beryl spent a lot of time making sure she felt special. I should have guessed she'd be at the Ball. She was definitely Someone with a capital S.

'Hey, Della,' Kevin said. 'How's Matthew Strange?'

Della's lips pressed together into a thin line. 'He's going to be fine,' she said. Most people would have thought Della was angry, but I knew better. My sister was scared, and she was trying to hide it.

'Alice,' she said. 'We need to talk.'

CHAPTER 3

'Would you like some cocoa?' I asked as Della hung up her coat. 'I can make another cup.'

Della checked to make sure the door was locked and peeked out through the blinds into the street. 'Dairy is awful for my voice. I'll have tea. With lemon,' she said over her shoulder. Then she turned to look at me. 'Where's Dad?'

'Chasing down a lead. He said he'll call you later.'

'OK, good.' Della nodded. She checked the street again.

Kevin gave me a look that said *what's going on?* I just shrugged and put the kettle on. Della had a bad habit of milking things for drama, but even I had to admit she looked really worried.

'Well, if she's having tea, she doesn't need these,' Kevin said. He helped himself to the last two marshmallows in the bag and leant against the counter, slurping his cocoa.

'Help yourself,' Della said, sitting down at the counter. Della loved marshmallows, even if she didn't want cocoa. Something was definitely not right.

I poured out the tea and handed Della some honey and a squeezy bottle of lemon juice from the back of the fridge.

Della raised a disapproving eyebrow. 'You don't have real lemons?'

'It's the middle of February. Not exactly lemonade season.'

Della sighed, like the weight of the entire world had just gotten one degree heavier. But she used the bottle. Her spoon clinked against the side of the mug as she stirred and the smell of lemon and honey filled the air.

'So what's this all about?' I asked after she took her first sip.

Della took a deep breath and looked over her shoulder, as if someone might have snuck in while she wasn't looking.

'Della, no one's going to spy on us.'

My sister licked her lips and looked over my shoulder, then looked back at me. Kevin and I both leant closer, waiting for her to hurry up and spill the beans.

'I want to hire you,' she said.

I rocked back and almost fell off my seat. Out of the corner of my eye, Kevin rubbed his hands together, his smile growing like a weed.

'Excuse me?' I asked once I had my balance back.

Della looked at me hard. If it had been the usual kind of

favour, she'd have given me her best earnest eyes and pleading smile. But she wasn't acting at all.

'You heard me, I want to hire you.'

'Hire me to do what?' I asked slowly.

My sister paused, building dramatic tension.

'Della, what's going on?' I asked.

'Don't laugh,' she said. 'Either of you.'

I nodded. Kevin drew an X over his heart.

'I think the Beryl is haunted.'

I started to stand up. I knew my sister could be superstitious, but this was ridiculous.

Della grabbed the hem of my sleeve and pulled me back down. 'I'm serious,' she said. 'And it isn't just me. Everyone can feel it.'

'Della, that's crazy. Besides,' I went on quickly when I saw the look on my sister's face, 'what's the big deal? Aren't all theatres haunted?'

'Of course they are, but those are friendly ghosts. The spirits of actors who perform at night. They'd never mess with the set or do anything to hurt the show.'

I closed my eyes and counted up in primes. Della was upset and I didn't want to laugh at her, but it was ridiculous. There are no such things as ghosts.

Della kept right on talking. 'This ghost is different. It's trying to ruin the show. It's evil.'

I sighed. 'Look, Della. I know you're upset about knocking over the safe, but blaming a ghost . . .'

'I didn't knock it over,' Della said sharply. '*Something* made the door stick. And *something* got it loose from the floor. That definitely wasn't me.'

I paused. She wasn't totally wrong. Someone had prised the safe up from the floor, and that had probably warped the door, making it stick. But it was some*one* not some*thing*.

I opened my mouth, but Della was already moving on, waving her hands at me, like she was erasing a line of unimportant details from a chalkboard.

'It isn't just the safe falling. I was at the Beryl for a week before your school break started, and things have been going wrong since the moment we stepped through that door.'

'Like what?' Kevin asked, before I could tell him not to encourage her.

Della leant forward, both hands flat on the counter. 'At first it was just small things, like the props weren't where they were supposed to be. Or set pieces breaking. Then the curtain started jamming. And the lights.' She shivered. 'They're always flickering.'

'Della, the wiring in that place is ancient.'

Della tossed her hair and gave me a look that could have withered a cactus. I stopped talking.

'It's just . . .' Della struggled to find the right words. 'It's just *too much*. Every day it's something else. And now it's almost killed our lead actor. I'm scared what will happen next. You have to believe me!'

I rubbed at my temples and tried to force away the fog. Della wasn't going to take no for an answer. Besides, what if she was right? Not about the ghost – there was no way I was buying that. But if things really did keep going wrong, maybe there was something else going on behind the scenes at the Beryl?

Della's phone chimed and she glanced at the screen. 'That's Mom,' she said. She took a deep breath. 'Alice, please. I need your help.'

It was the 'please' that got me.

'All right,' I said. 'All right, let's say you're right. What do you want me to do about it?'

'What do you think? I want you to find out who the ghost is and stop it.'

I raised an eyebrow. Kevin grinned.

'What?' Della said, grabbing her coat and tugging it back on. Outside a car horn honked. Mom was in a hurry. 'We need to know who the angry spirit is and what it wants in order to appease it.'

'You've got to be kidding me,' I mumbled, holding my head in my hands.

Kevin smacked the counter in excitement. 'This is awesome.'

I glared at him. He wasn't helping at all. 'There are no such things as ghosts.'

Della drew in a deep breath and scowled at me, crossing her arms. She tipped her head to one side, and I could see her scheming. She gave a curt nod and looked me straight in the eye. 'Fine,' she said with a sniff. 'Prove it.'

'Excuse me?' I asked.

Kevin clenched his fist in silent celebration. I hated to admit it, but he knew me. And Della knew exactly what she was doing. I'd never be able to say it wasn't a ghost 'just because' and leave it at that.

'Things are going wrong, Alice. That's a fact. Forget I said a ghost was doing it and find out who the "real" culprit is.'

I looked at Della, then sighed. All I'd wanted to do this February break was plant myself on the couch with a mug of hot chocolate and my copy of *Fermat's Last Theorem*. But it looked like I'd be stuck digging up dirt instead. I rubbed at the skin between my eyebrows and sighed.

'All right,' I said. 'I'll look into it.'

'I knew you'd help! You're the best.' Della practically vibrated with excitement. She threw her arms around me in a giant hug. 'You too, Kevin. Make sure she keeps an open mind.'

Kevin stood up and actually saluted my sister.

'Wait,' I said, before the two of them could get too far. 'I'll only take the case if I get to do things my way. That means no hassling me every five minutes to see if I've solved it yet.'

'Got it.' Della drew a cross over her heart.

'And don't go telling everyone I'm investigating. Especially not Mom.'

I'd fallen off a first-storey fire escape on my last case. Ever since then, she's been more than a little over-protective.

Della's eyes went wide, her mouth opened into a perfect O of *who, me?*

'And when I prove there's no ghost, you have to believe me and not keep asking about it.'

'*If* you prove it.' Della swept the front door open and waved at us like a queen dismissing her court before stepping out into the night. She tossed me one last award-winning smile over her shoulder. '*If.*'

For a minute I thought about following her out to say goodnight to Mom, but it had started snowing again and the cold air made me shiver. I waved at the car instead and quickly shut the door, promising myself I'd go see Mom first thing in the morning.

'So,' Kevin said, rubbing his hands together, 'we're going on a ghost hunt.'

I groaned. 'You can't be serious.'

'Oh, come on. I've always wanted to see a ghost. And you told your sister you'd take the case.'

'I told Della I'd find out who's causing the problems at the Beryl. For all I know the culprit could be rats.'

'Whatever,' Kevin said. He dug around in the bottom of the takeaway bag and pulled out two fortune cookies, tossing one in my direction. 'We're on the case, so where do we start?'

'We?'

'Yes, *we*. You'd never have solved your last case without my help. You need me.'

I crossed my arms. The last time Kevin helped me on a case, he'd ended up with a compound fracture and I'd spent my summer pushing him around in a wheelchair.

'You just want to hang out with Matthew Strange.'

'Not true. I want to solve a mystery and save the Beryl.' Kevin hit me with his best angel impression. 'If I get to hang out with my favourite movie star of all time, that's just an added bonus.'

I started to say no, but then I thought about how much work I had to do to help get the Beryl ready for opening night. If I was going to have enough time to investigate as well, I'd need some help. Besides, it might be nice to have a non-theatre buff around.

'Fine,' I said, caving in. 'But the case is a secret. So you'll have to help me with the cleaning and anything else Mom and Linda come up with. And I really mean help, not stand there and wisecrack.'

Kevin crossed his finger over his heart and held up his hand. 'Scout's honour.'

'And no stalking Matthew Strange, or doing anything weird.'

'You have my word.'

I didn't believe him for a minute.

CHAPTER 4

I woke up early the next morning with the covers pulled tight under my chin. The sky was still dark outside my window, but the smell of coffee drifted up from the kitchen. Dad must have gotten up early, or maybe he hadn't gone to bed at all. I pulled the duvet off the bed and wrapped it around my shoulders as I stumbled downstairs.

The living room was even colder than my bedroom. I pulled the duvet tighter as I poured myself some coffee and stuck a slice of bread in the toaster. Judging from the amount left in the pot, Dad would need a refill too. I poured him a fresh cup and added three spoons of sugar. Then I shuffled my way to his office.

'Morning, sweetie,' Dad said without slowing down. He was still wearing his waiter outfit, his bow tie unhooked and dangling from his collar. A small orange stain marred the front of his shirt. 'Can you pour me another cup of coffee? I want to get all this down while it's still fresh.'

'You look happy,' I said, holding out the fresh mug. 'Did you get your interview with Cragthorne?'

Dad switched to typing one-handed long enough to grab the mug, take a sip and then stick it on the bullseye stain to the right of his keyboard, shoving his other empty mug out of the way. Dad's the only person I know who can type and talk about two different things at the same time.

'Not even close. The man spent the whole night yelling at people on his phone. But that's OK,' Dad smiled, 'something even better happened.'

I raised an eyebrow, inviting him to tell me more. I knew he'd tell me anyway, but there was no reason not to be polite.

'One of the Astor cousins was robbed.'

'That's good?'

'Good? It's *sensational!* The thief took the sapphires right off her neck and she never felt a thing. A very professional job. And the victim's an Astor. They're always front-page news.'

I guess, being a crime reporter meant Dad's idea of a good night out was a little warped. I sat down on the edge of the desk and watched him type.

'What are you up to today?' he asked.

'The Beryl.' I took a sip of coffee and waited for it to

warm me from the inside out.

'Ah,' Dad said. 'The poor old Beryl, but I think something else is up, isn't it? My source at the hospital said *both* of your stars paid them a visit last night. What's going on?'

Dad wasn't the best crime reporter at the *Philadelphia Daily News* for nothing. He could sniff out a story three blocks away and buried under a block of ice.

'I told you, it was just a small accident,' I said. Dad waited. He could tell something else was bothering me. 'Della thinks the place is haunted. She wants me to see if I can find out who the ghost is.'

'Any leads?'

'Very funny, Dad. There are no such things as ghosts.'

'True, but your sister's no slouch. If she thinks something is going on, it probably is. She is a Jones, after all.'

Dad wiggled his eyebrows at me, and I had to admit he was right. That safe hadn't prised itself loose. I took a bite of toast. I needed more facts.

'There.' He leant back in his chair, stretching his arms over his head and yawning. 'I'm beat. Are you OK to get to the theatre?'

My mouth was full of toast so I just nodded. It was only a twenty-minute bike ride, and braving the cold seemed a lot smarter than letting my sleep-deprived dad get behind the wheel. He drove enough like a maniac when fully rested.

Dad stood up, grimaced and massaged the small of his

back. 'Well then, I'm going to hit the sack. I've got another party tonight. If I'm lucky maybe I'll get to interview Cragthorne *and* catch a thief.'

'Maybe Cragthorne *is* the thief,' I joked.

'Ha, if only. Now that would be a story.' He paused for a moment, imagining the headline. Then he ruffled his hand through my hair. 'Have a nice dinner with your mom tonight. And tell your sister to come see me when she has a chance.'

'I will, Dad. Go to bed.'

'OK, sweetie, whatever you say.' He kissed me on the forehead and then slumped upstairs.

I was just getting comfortable on the couch with my book and a second cup of coffee when my phone rang.

'Alice, it's Mom.'

'Hi, Mom,' I said. 'Is everything OK?'

'Of course, everything is fine. Linda and I just have a little job for you and I was hoping you could come in early today.'

I sighed. *Fermat's Last Theorem* would have to wait.

It was barely seven o'clock, and the sun was just peeking over the tops of the buildings as I cycled into town. The cold wind stung my face. Subway steam hung over the grates in low dense clouds of fog. I turned north on 8th Street, pedalling hard and fast, and soon I was sweating inside my coat.

The Beryl was on the very edge of Old City, past Philly's

more famous landmarks. Maybe that was one of the reasons it had been allowed to fall apart. Out of sight out of mind. I pulled up short on the corner across from the theatre. Kevin was standing with his back against the wall, blowing on his hands and stamping his feet, trying to keep warm. I'd texted him before I left, but I hadn't thought he'd beat me there.

He waved and walked towards me as I pulled up on to the pavement. His cheeks and nose looked like stop signs against the cold white of the rest of his skin.

'How long have you been here?' I asked.

'I don't know, not too long,' he said, shivering. He looked like he was about to die of exposure.

'You should have waited in the Seven–Eleven.' I shrugged in the direction of the shop as I crouched down and wrapped my bike chain around the lamppost and through the frame of my bike.

'I did, but the guy behind the counter kept giving me the evil eye.'

The metal slipped through my gloves and I grimaced, pulling them off with my teeth. 'Yeah, I don't think he likes kids.'

The lock was so cold it stuck to my fingers, just enough to pull off a layer of skin. I jerked my hand back and shook it, and that's when I spotted the bike propped up against the Beryl. A figure in a black puffy coat stood beside it and a strange clacking sound filled the air.

I don't know if it was the cold or the fact that I didn't get enough sleep the night before, or that Kevin kept asking me questions about Matthew Strange, but it took me a few seconds to put two and two together. That clacking was the sound of someone shaking a can of spray paint.

'Hey!' I shouted, and ran across the street, leaving Kevin open-mouthed behind me.

I pulled my phone out of my pocket and fumbled to turn on the camera with frozen fingers. I'd already spent three afternoons scrubbing graffiti off the Beryl's walls. A great streak of neon blue appeared on the side of the building and the smell of paint hit me hard. I held up my phone and started recording – even if the culprit got away, at least I'd have evidence.

'What do you think you're doing?' I yelled.

I don't know what surprised me more, the fact that he threw the can at me or that I actually caught it. As I stood there dumbfounded, the kid raced forward and snatched my phone from where I'd dropped it on the ground, then sprinted back towards his bike.

'Hey,' I shouted again, and ran after him. My face felt red and it had nothing to do with the cold. I couldn't believe I'd been so sloppy.

I'm not the fastest runner, but I was at least fifteen centimetres taller than the kid. I sprinted up the pavement with everything I had, each stride closing the gap between us. I could hear Kevin yelling somewhere behind me.

The kid was just a few paces ahead of me now. I could hear his feet crunching the ice on the pavement. His hood flapped against his back with every step. I reached out. My fingers brushed against its fake fur trim and then closed on air. I told my screaming lungs to shut up and ran harder. This time my hand closed down on the hood and I pulled hard.

Which would have been great – if I hadn't chosen that moment to step on a patch of black ice.

My foot slipped and my stomach clenched as I lost my balance. I gripped the hood tighter, hoping it would keep me from wiping out, but I'm not that lucky. The kid slipped out of the too-big sleeves and I hit the ground hard, concrete scraping at my palms and chin.

I rolled over in time to see the kid slow down to look at me. He actually smiled. Then he grabbed his bike from the alley and took off right at me, one hand on the handlebars, the other on a brand new spray can, unleashing a livid green stripe along the Beryl's wall.

I rolled out of the way, but Kevin held his ground. He stood in the middle of the pavement, arms spread wide, trying to block the bike's path. The graffiti bandit didn't slow down – he didn't stop spraying either. Kevin's eyes widened, and he dived to the side, flattening himself against the wall of the Beryl just in time to avoid being struck by the speeding bicycle.

I heard the kid laughing, a high gloating sound. Then he

tucked the spray can into the water-bottle holder on his bike, shifted down a gear and sped away up the street.

Kevin coughed and spluttered, spitting bright green flecks into the snowbank. He'd gotten his hands up to cover his face just in time. The kid didn't stop spraying for anyone.

'That brat. I'll kill him!' Kevin spluttered.

He had speckles of bright green paint on his hat and face where the spray had gotten around his hands. His gloves were completely limed. Behind him I could just make out the words *Beware the Curse*.

I pushed myself on to my feet and brushed off my palms. 'Are you OK?'

Kevin spat into the snow and looked at his bright green gloves. 'These were brand-new. My mom's gonna kill me.'

CHAPTER

5

I found Mom in the costume workshop, kneeling beside a low tailor's stool, her pale pink hair pulled back in a neat French twist. Standing on the stool was Vivian Rollins, wearing a Victorian day dress and oversized sunglasses. She massaged her temples in small, tragic circles while Mom pinned up the hem.

'Hi, honey,' Mom said around a mouthful of pins. She had at least twenty of the things held fast between her scarlet lips. 'Thanks for coming in early today. I just need to—'

Her eyes widened and she almost lost the pins as she caught sight of Kevin.

'What on earth happened?' she asked through tight lips.

'I got in the way of some punk spray-painting the front of the theatre,' Kevin said before I could stop him. Mom always imagines the worst-case scenario.

'It was just a kid, Mom. Nothing dangerous,' I said quickly.

Mom crossed her arms.

'I'm serious. He can't have been older than ten.'

Her arms stayed crossed, but her shoulders relaxed just a touch.

Kevin shuffled into the room, peeling off his green-speckled coat. He reached for a spare hanger on the costume rack.

'Ah,' Mom held up her hand. 'Painted people stay away from the costumes. Neon green is *not* a period colour.'

'Sorry, Ms Lynn,' Kevin said, his angel act not working quite so well covered in green, but my mom still softened.

'Leave your coat here, Kevin. I'll see what I can do to get the paint out.'

Vivian sighed heavily.

'I'm almost done, Vivian dear. Just a few more and then you can get down.'

Vivian took a deep breath and nodded bravely, waiting for someone to ask her what was wrong. She probably still felt upstaged since Matthew Strange was the one who got all the attention at the hospital. Of course, he'd been the one who'd actually been injured, but that wouldn't matter to Vivian.

I chose to ignore her.

I flopped down on the couch in the corner. Kevin

paused, waiting to see if Mom would object to painted people touching the couch. She didn't.

Mom shuffled around the circumference of Vivian's full skirt, securing it with the last of her pins. The she stood up and arched her back. She must have been bent over for a while because I could hear her spine pop.

'OK, Vivian, you're all set. You can take it off now.'

Kevin's face went so red I could see it through the paint. Even Vivian noticed. She smiled for the first time since we'd arrived and then disappeared to change behind an old folding screen in the corner of the room.

'Ouch,' Mom said, rolling her shoulders. 'Next time I'll design costumes for a nice modern play. These crinoline skirts are going to be the death of me.'

'The dress looks great,' I said.

Mom beamed at me. 'You know, while you're here, you should let me do a fitting. I found an amazing electric-blue silk that would look stunning with your hair.'

I cringed. Mom was determined to design a red-carpet-worthy dress for me to wear on opening night. I'm more of a jeans and T-shirt kind of girl, but Mom insisted and I hadn't been able to bring myself to say no.

'Maybe later,' I said, and tried to change the subject. 'What was the job you wanted me to do?'

Mom gave me a hard look and I got the message. I wasn't going to get out of it that easily.

'I'll tell you while I'm measuring.'

'Yeah, Alice,' Kevin said. 'She can tell you while she measures.'

My palms started to itch. The last thing I wanted was Kevin giving my mom 'helpful' suggestions about her designs.

'It will take two minutes, less if you stand still and don't fidget.'

There was no getting out of it. I climbed up on to the small stool and held out my arms.

'That's better.'

'So what is this job?' I asked as Mom stretched her measuring tape across my shoulders. Kevin sat on the couch with his arms behind his head, grinning at me like a sideshow attraction. I looked up at the ceiling and counted up in primes, fighting the urge to make a run for it.

'Do you remember how the east side of the theatre has been off limits until now?'

I nodded. The east side of the building was where the fire started back in the twenties.

'Well, the builders have finally given us the all clear to go back in. Linda and I had a nose around last night, and we found a storeroom.' Her eyes practically sparkled. 'Some-one must have tried to clean up after the fire, before the building was shut down. It's just full of treasures from the Beryl's past.' Mom paused, jotting numbers in the little notebook where she drew her designs. I caught a glimpse of something frilly and short and clenched my teeth hoping it wasn't meant for me.

'And . . .?' I said carefully.

'And Linda and I thought, since you weren't doing anything else, you could sort through the old boxes. Pull out some of the more interesting pieces. We'd like you to set up a display in the lobby. Something about the history of the Beryl. Something to make it seem a little less' – she paused looking for the right word – 'bare.'

I knew what she meant. The Save the Beryl campaign had raised a lot of money, but it had all gone on making the building safe. There wasn't much left for carpets, and fancy paint.

Mom stood up, snapping her notebook shut. 'There, that wasn't so difficult now, was it?'

I stepped off the stool, ignoring Kevin's smirk.

Mom took a chain from around her neck and held it out to me. A large, old-fashioned key swung from the end. 'Here. I think the detective in you will find it very interesting. Uncovering the mysteries of the Beryl.'

'It's funny you should say that,' Kevin said.

Mom turned to look at him and I made desperate *don't say anything* signs behind her back. If Mom knew I was looking into the trouble at the Beryl, the case would be over before it began.

Kevin didn't miss a beat. 'Alice was telling me all about the fire that ruined the Beryl back in the twenties. I'm here to help.'

Mom beamed. 'Wonderful. It's so good to see the next generation showing an interest in the theatrical history of the city.'

I thought about pointing out that Kevin was more interested in Matthew Strange than the Beryl, but settled on telling Mom how much Kevin loved tidying up instead.

Kevin looked at me like I'd accused him of enjoying stewed prunes.

'Come on, Mr Clean, I'll show you where the bathroom is so you can wash your face before we get started.'

'You don't think you're going to get that paint off with soap, do you?' Vivian asked, peering over the top of her sunglasses. She'd come out from behind the screen wearing a black turtleneck and leggings, her costume draped over one arm.

'What else would he use?'

Vivian looked at the ceiling, begging the theatrical gods for patience. I guess, since no one was letting her play the tragic heroine, she'd recast herself as the helpful fairy godmother.

'Come with me, this way.' She sighed wearily and pushed the sunglasses back up her nose. Then Vivian handed Mom the dress and led the way out the door.

'I'll let Linda know you two are working on the display. Have fun!' Mom called as we ran out the door, trying to keep up with Vivian's long strides.

I shouldn't have hurried. Vivian stopped cold in the

theatre door and I just barely stopped in time to avoid running into her. Kevin didn't have time to stop at all and he ran into me, pushing all three of us into the dark theatre.

Vivian stood perfectly still. Her spine was stiff and straight. The theatre was too dark to see more than the outline of her face, but I could tell she was scared.

'What's wrong?' I asked.

'The ghost light,' Vivian whispered. Kevin heard the word 'ghost' and he leant eagerly over my shoulder, squinting into the darkness. I jabbed him with my elbow. The last thing I needed was him encouraging Vivian.

She pointed one long elegant finger towards the stage. 'The ghost light isn't on.' She tugged the sunglasses from her face and looked around the empty theatre, like she expected a whole cast of spirits to start swirling out of the walls.

I shook my head. Just what I needed, another actor who believed the Beryl was haunted.

'Pete probably turned it off earlier,' I said.

Vivian didn't look convinced.

'What's a ghost light?' Kevin whispered.

'We leave it on for the spirits of actors past,' Vivian said. 'So they can perform at night. If the theatre goes dark, the spirits cause trouble. And I've never been in a show with more trouble.' She shivered and wrapped her arms around herself. I could practically see her replaying yesterday's accident. All that was missing was the flash-back strum of a harp.

Della had been right. She wasn't the only one who thought the Beryl was having more problems than usual.

Vivian spun in a circle three times, curtsied towards the stage and spat over her shoulder, then she hurried down the aisle, walking past the stage without looking up.

Kevin and I followed Vivian carefully through the dark-ened theatre. The builders had lined the aisle with small strips of reflective tape and they glinted in the low light, guiding us safely to the bottom of the theatre and around the steep drop into the orchestra pit.

Vivian led us to the dressing room she shared with Della, a small neat space which was surprisingly modern. The only furniture from before the fire was an old make-up table, the kind with a large mirror surrounded by lights. Vivian dragged Kevin in front of it and pushed him into a metal folding chair.

'Here,' she said, handing him a small jar of white face cream, her tone overly bright. 'If it takes off stage make-up, it'll take off anything.'

Kevin looked at me for help, but it was already too late. Vivian sensed his hesitation and unscrewed the lid herself. The smell of lily of the valley filled the dressing room as she slathered his face in cold cream.

'So what kind of trouble has the play had?' I asked.

Vivian tossed her hair over her shoulder. 'What kind of

trouble *hasn't* it had?'

'Anything specific?' I asked. I couldn't investigate vague suspicions.

'Well, last week the heel of my shoe snapped and I almost fell down the stairs. Linda was furious because the shoe was part of the costume from the original production. She didn't seem to care that *I* almost broke my neck. And then there was what happened yesterday.'

Vivian spread another layer of cream across Kevin's forehead and rubbed it into his skin. Her fingers shook slightly, sending little specks of cream on to the shoulder of his coat.

'I could have been killed. I'm supposed to lean on that safe in the next scene. She wants me to die . . .' The last words were a whisper.

'Who is *she*?' I asked.

Vivian looked around, as if someone might be listening, then leant in close. 'It's Kittie Grace. She's jealous that I've taken her part. She's trying to destroy me.'

I frowned. 'Do you really think someone would try to hurt you because you beat them for a part in the show? You aren't even getting paid.'

Vivian looked at me like I was something that had crawled out from behind the refrigerator.

'Kittie Grace was the actress who played my role in the original production of *The Curse*. She died on opening night, in the fire that ruined the Beryl. Don't you see?'

Vivian's well-trained voice filled the small room, while her fingers were tight on Kevin's chin. 'She's angry and she wants revenge.'

I did my best not to pull a face, but it was just so ridiculous. Vivian opened her mouth to say more and then shut it again, her cheeks colouring slightly. She could probably tell that I didn't believe her. I tried to stop looking so sceptical, but Vivian was done talking.

She stood up and turned to the dresser without looking at me. Her body language was about as subtle as an elephant in a swimsuit. It practically shouted *you'll see, and then you'll be sorry.*

CHAPTER

6

'So?' Kevin asked when we were safely down the hall. His face was pink and paint-free and glowed like something out of a soap commercial. 'What do you think?'

'About what?'

'About Kittie Grace?'

I rolled my eyes and kept walking. The dressing rooms were on the west side of the Beryl, so we had to go back through the theatre before we could start sorting out the storeroom for Mom.

'I think there are no such things as ghosts,' I said.

'Come on, Alice. I thought you were going to keep an open mind. Kittie Grace sounds super-spooky.'

'Vivian could make a loaf of bread sound spooky. The only new fact she told us was that her heel broke. But if it was a shoe from the original production' – I did a quick calculation – 'it was at least ninety years old.'

'OK, but what if it wasn't an accident? You know, what's the probability of that many "accidents" happening in one show?'

Kevin raised an eyebrow as if to say checkmate. I should have never offered to tutor him in maths. But he had a point. If the safe wasn't an accident, there was a good chance the shoe wasn't either. I needed to talk to Pete. If the stage manager had a reasonable explanation for why the safe was loose, maybe I could put this whole case to bed.

I shouldered open the door into the theatre and blinked. The stage lights were on now. Pete must have been in the lighting booth getting ready for rehearsal. And the area bustled with activity.

Mom and Linda stood next to lobby doors at the top of the house as a quartet of removal men tried to manoeuvre a very large ball of bubble wrap into the room. Linda held the door open with one hand and held her smartphone in the other, typing furiously. Jarvis, the creepy caretaker, leant against the wall, watching them with a fierce scowl. He didn't trust outsiders. Actually, he didn't trust insiders much either. The way he watched the cast and crew made him look like a cop at a cat burglar convention.

Della caught sight of us and waved Kevin and me over.

'What's going on?' I asked, nodding to the doorway.

'Irinke,' Della said with a heavy accent. 'She bought us a chandelier at the Liberty Ball silent auction last night.'

One of the removal men stumbled slightly and the package slipped dangerously close to the floor.

'Careful with that!' screeched a voice from outside the door. 'That's Austrian crystal!'

I took a step to one side and caught sight of Irinke in the doorway behind the removal men, wrapped head to toe in grey-blue fur. Her hand clutched the neck of her coat like a jewel-encrusted claw. Della said Irinke was a direct descendant of the dukes of Transylvania. I didn't think it was that impressive, since Transylvania wasn't a separate country any more. But I guess royalty is for ever.

Mom moved out of the doorway and took Irinke by the arm, trying to keep her calm. It didn't work.

'I said, *be careful*!' Irinke shrieked again, making everyone in the room jump. She twisted her arm out of Mom's grasp in a surprisingly lithe motion.

Linda winced, but her thumb on her smartphone didn't slow down. 'Irinke, you really didn't need to go to all this trouble,' she said as the men finally angled the parcel through the door.

'Nonsense. I insist. You can't reopen this beautiful building without an equally beautiful chandelier.' Irinke slid into the theatre. 'Ashley, Ashley,' she snapped and a small rabbit-faced man stepped out of her shadow. 'Make yourself useful and *watch* them.' She gestured at the removal men.

Ashley jerked his head in a small nod and started to walk away.

Irinke cleared her throat and he stopped.

'Is there something else, Auntie Irinke?'

Irinke looked at him the way you look on your shoe after you step in dog poo. 'My coat.' She held out her arms and Ashley rushed to assist. Then he folded it over his arm and walked back to the removal men.

'I'm so sorry, I promised his mother I'd look after him. But he's useless, really,' Irinke said to the room in general. If she noticed the uncomfortable silence, she didn't care. She clapped excitedly as the removal men began to unwrap the first layer of bubble wrap.

'As soon as I saw this at the silent auction, I simply *had* to win it for you. It's not as grand as the chandelier at the Palace of Arts. I danced there, in my youth.'

I rolled my eyes. Irinke never missed a chance to tell people she used to be a ballerina.

'But it is *perfect* for this space. Wait till you see it. You won't be able to contain yourself. The men will install it, so there's nothing to worry about.'

Linda smiled graciously, then she spotted me. 'While we're waiting, Irinke, let me introduce Alice. She's the girl I was telling you about before. Virginia's daughter.'

'Alice, my darling,' Irinke said, drawing out the word *darling* like it was toffee. 'Linda tells me you are the lucky child who gets to go treasure hunting through the Beryl's past.' Irinke's eyes glittered under heavy lids. I could feel Kevin perk up beside me at the word *treasure*.

'I haven't found anything yet,' I said quickly. There was something about the way she watched me that made my skin crawl.

'Don't sell yourself short, my dear. The first rule of theatre is self-promotion.' She stepped a little closer to me and the heavy scent of her perfume filled my nose. 'Self-promotion and presentation. I was just telling Linda that my jeweller has a few spare display cases she's offered to let us use. For your display. Isn't that wonderful?'

To be honest, I hadn't thought that far ahead. I didn't even know if there'd be anything worth presenting.

Linda answered before I had a chance to speak. 'You do too much for us, Irinke,' she said. 'How will we ever be able to repay you?'

'It's no worry. I'm happy to do what I can for this beautiful old building. I do so want to see it returned to its past glory.'

Linda beamed. 'I'm sure Alice would be happy to give you a tour. Once she and her friend have cleaned it up a bit, of course.'

Irinke turned to me, her lips quirked up into an odd smile, like she'd seen something funny but she was the only one who got the joke. 'Thank you, my dear. I would enjoy that very much.'

'Well, I guess we'd better get started then,' I said,

backing away. Irinke gave me the creeps.

She smiled again and nodded, granting me permission to leave. I practically bolted, with Kevin close on my heels.

'Who was *that*?'

'That's Irinke Barscay,' Della said, and I jumped.

'Della!' I said, trying to stuff my heart back into my chest.

'Don't mind her,' Kevin said. 'We just found out about the ghost of Kittie Grace.'

Della's face went waxy and pale. I could have killed him. Kevin thought ghost hunting was fun, but Della was really scared.

'He doesn't mean it,' I said hurriedly. 'Vivian thinks Kittie Grace is out to get her because she took her part in the play. But she's wrong.'

Della sniffed. 'Are you sure? Do you have proof?'

I sighed. I hadn't wanted to tell Della about the gouges in the floor, not until I'd talked to Pete. But it was the only way I could think of to make her see that whatever was causing the problems, it was someone with a body.

'Look, you know I don't believe in ghosts,' I said. Della opened her mouth but I kept talking before she could interrupt me. 'But I do believe in you, Della, OK? I'm keeping an open mind and gathering real facts. Someone tampered with that safe. And you aren't the only one who's noticed things going wrong. I'll get to the bottom of it, I promise. But you only asked me to look into it last night.'

Della's shoulders slumped and my sister suddenly looked very tired. I hadn't realized how much this show meant to her. I felt a sudden rush of anger at whoever was making my sister feel so scared.

'There's only four more days till opening night,' she said. 'You need to figure out whoever, whatever, is doing this and stop them before it's too late.'

'Don't worry,' I said. 'I will.'

CHAPTER 7

The storeroom was at the very back of the theatre where the fuel for the Beryl's dangerous gas-powered lights had been kept back in the 1900s. After the fire, I guess someone figured it would be more use as a storeroom, but they hadn't gotten rid of the network of pipes that carried the gas to the stage.

'Wow,' Kevin said from behind me. 'Movie stars and ghosts, this is the best holiday ever.'

I shot him a look that said *keep your voice down*. The remnants of the engineers' DO NOT ENTER tape fluttered from the wall and the smell of soot grew stronger along with the scent of new wood and paint. Kevin lowered his voice and kept talking.

'I wonder if we'll see it? Maybe we should stake out the theatre at night?'

'No, because there isn't anything to see.'

'Spoilsport.'

I stopped in front of the storeroom door. The words GAS HOUSE were painted across it in faded gold letters. Kevin snorted and I fished out my key quickly before he could start cracking jokes. The lock stuck and I had to jiggle the handle a few times before it turned. The hinges were ancient and creaked horribly.

Inside, it looked like a bomb had gone off. Boxes, trunks, hatboxes, garment bags, bits of sets, paintings and playbills, old mouldering make-up and annotated scripts. It had all been shoved in through the door and left wherever it landed. Everything was coated in greasy layers of soot and cobwebs that seemed to seep into my skin.

'Why do I always end up in places like this when we hang out?' Kevin asked.

'I guess you're just lucky,' I said. 'At least there's no rotten food, right?' I lifted the corner of one of the trunks and a puff of ancient dust wafted out.

Kevin wrinkled his nose and shuddered. 'Thank goodness for small favours,' he said. 'You're going to tell Matthew Strange how helpful I am, right?'

'I thought you agreed, no stalking.'

'I'm not stalking. I'm part of the crew. Besides, I gave him first aid. We're practically best friends now.'

I bit back a smile. I had to admit, having Kevin around made the Beryl a lot more entertaining.

I took a deep breath, and immediately regretted it. A fun little job, my foot. We'd need a year to sort through all this. And a hazmat suit. And Mom wanted a lobby display by opening night? I shoved my dismay back into my shoes. Standing around moaning wasn't going to help. We'd just have to do our best and hope we got lucky.

'Pick a box and start sorting,' I said. 'We'll put anything good on that table over there, and the rest can go in the back corner.'

'Table good. Corner bad. Got it.'

I dug through my bag and pulled out a notebook and pen so we could catalogue our findings and label the boxes we'd already searched. If I had my phone, I could have taken pictures. I ground my teeth.

'What's wrong?' Kevin asked as he hefted a canvas shoe box on to the table in front of me.

'I can't believe I lost my phone.'

'Your dad knows the police, can't he get them to track it down for you?' Kevin blew a cloud of dust off the top of the box and lifted the lid.

I was expecting a pair of shoes. Instead, the box was full of papers – business letters and bills, all yellow and brittle under my fingertips. It would probably be interesting to a theatre historian, but I didn't think it had the 'pizzazz' Linda was looking for.

'The police have more important things to do than find my mobile,' I said as I thumbed through the papers. We were going to need another pile for the things that were too boring for the display, but not bad enough to toss.

'I guess it's up to us then.'

'Excuse me?' I pulled the last stack of papers out of the box. They looked like some sort of loan agreement for something called the Midnight Star. I stuck them in the 'boring' pile.

'You said you've already cleaned the front of the theatre three times. So the spray-painting brat keeps coming back. If that's true, then all we need to do to get your phone back is be there the next time he strikes.'

He was right. I couldn't believe I hadn't figured it out myself. I'd been so busy trying to convince Della that ghosts weren't real, I hadn't given the graffiti bandit more than a passing thought.

'Besides,' Kevin said, clearly loving his new role as lead detective, 'don't you want to know *why* he keeps tagging the Beryl? It's not normal to keep coming back to the same spot. It isn't even normal graffiti. I mean, "Beware the Curse". What's that all about?'

I shrugged. 'He probably just saw the name of the play on the marquee out front and thought it would be funny.'

Kevin didn't look convinced.

'But you're right, we should try to catch him. I'm sick of scrubbing bricks.'

Kevin staggered and clutched at his chest like I'd shocked him into a heart attack.

'Come on, these boxes aren't going to unpack themselves,' I said, before he could get too carried away.

Kevin grinned and grabbed another box, dragging it to the centre of the room. 'Oh, this one's heavy. I've got a good feeling about this.'

The box was full of moth-eaten costumes, most of them were more holes than fabric. Although one blue ballgown had just about survived, if you could ignore the smell. The box after that was full of dirty rags and it got worse from there. Strips of musty fabric, melted stubs of candles, cast-off cuts of wood, old dried and crusted tins of paint, everything covered in soot and grime. In one corner, we found an old feather pillow and a pile of blankets that had become infested with mice sometime in the past century. The mice were long gone, but several tiny skeletons remained. I shuddered violently as I kicked those into the 'to be burnt' pile.

The pillow felt too heavy against my foot and made an odd scraping sound. I picked it up by the corner, trying to touch as little of the filthy fabric as possible. A leather notebook smacked the floor with a sharp clap and a cloud of dust.

'What's that?' Kevin asked.

'It looks like a journal.'

The pages were brittle, but not singed or sooty. The inside cover bore the name *Franklin Oswald, 1927–1978* in small cramped cursive letters.

I flipped a few pages and tried to read.

I know it's still here. It must be here. If I had help it would take less time to search, but they can't be trusted. None of them can be trusted. They say the fire started it all, but I know what really happened. It was one of them. I'll find the Star myself. And once I find the Star, I'll rebuild and everything will be as it should.

Behind me, the door opened with a horrible screech of rusty hinges and I jumped, closing the book with an audible snap.

'Sorry, Alice,' Pete said. 'I didn't mean to startle you. Della told me you'd be here . . .' His voice trailed off and he stared into the room.

The Beryl's stage manager was a large man with a shiny bald head and a walrus moustache. He wore black jeans and a black T-shirt. The slogan *Keep Calm and Let the Stage Crew Handle It* stretched tight across his belly.

'Have you found anything yet?'

Kevin snorted.

'Nothing good,' I said.

Pete's eyes darted from one pile of boxes to the next, sparkling with dreams of finding original set pieces and bringing them back to the stage.

'Do you want to open a box?' I asked. It would be a lot easier to grill Pete about the accident with the safe if he was distracted by digging for historic gold.

Pete looked at me like I'd offered him a winning lottery ticket. 'Can I?' He didn't wait for me to answer, just barrelled into the room, drumming his fingers together as he weighed his options. He finally settled on a large crate near the door, sliding it across the floor towards the table. 'Oooh, it's heavy,' he said and cracked open the lid.

'Whoa,' Kevin said. 'It looks like a robot died in there.'

The box was full of metal tubes and cylinders and cracked rubber tubing. Loose nuts and bolts rattled in the bottom of the box, and scraps of scorched hessian were tucked between the gaps.

'No way,' Pete said, staring into the box with his jaw hanging open.

'What is it?'

'It's a limelight. An original limelight.' Pete started unloading the box like it was a Christmas stocking. 'It's all here. Even the lime.' He held up what looked like a small cube of brownish salt. 'See, the gas would go through these tubes and then when the flame reacted with the lime you'd get a brilliant white light. This was before electricity, of course.'

Kevin gave me a look over the top of Pete's head, asking if he was normal. I shrugged. Pete was passionate about preserving the history of the Beryl. He'd rebuilt the set of *The Curse* using as many original pieces as he could salvage and faithfully recreating anything he couldn't.

'So, Pete,' I asked casually, 'how's the set? Could you fix everything after the accident OK?'

Pete stopped unloading the box and looked at me. 'Thank you, Alice. You know, you're the only one who's asked. Everyone is always so concerned about the actors, but no one ever gives the set the credit it deserves.'

I nodded sympathetically and waited for him to continue.

'It wasn't tough to fix, just a bit of gorilla glue. That safe was from the original 1927 set. They knew how to build things back then. Solid as a rock.'

I cringed, imagining a rock crashing down on Matthew Strange's head.

'Was that why it fell? Wasn't it glued down?' Kevin asked.

'Of course it wasn't. It was nailed down. Everything on the top level is.' Pete stopped suddenly, his mouth hanging open. It just hit him: if the safe had been nailed down, how had it fallen?

My heart sank. So much for Pete having a reasonable explanation, although at this point I wasn't that surprised. The more I learnt, the more I was sure Della was right. Someone was trying to make a mess of things.

Pete lifted the casing of the limelight out of the box and held it out in front of him, his eyes practically glowing. 'I could rebuild this,' he said. 'An original limelight would look great in your display, don't you think?'

I nodded. It might not be what Linda was expecting, but

it was better than anything else we'd found so far.

I started to help Pete put the pieces back in the box when something strange caught my eye. I pushed a scrap of hessian aside, uncovering what looked like a blob of melted copper the size of a loaf of bread.

I lifted it up carefully, because as soon as I touched it, I knew it wasn't made of metal but glass.

'Oh wow, look at that,' Pete said. 'I've heard of vitrified sandbags, but I've never seen one before!'

Kevin scooted in behind me and jostled my shoulder. 'Sorry,' he said, and backed up a few centimetres.

Looking more carefully, Pete was right. The blob was shaped just like the sandbags I'd seen hanging backstage, the ones that counterbalanced the curtains and helped lift the set into the flies when it was time for a scene change. But instead of brown hessian, it had a beautiful iridescent shimmer. Pete held out his hands and I passed it to him carefully.

'What's vitrified?' Kevin asked.

'It means turned into glass. It's what happens when sand melts.' I held out my hands and Pete handed the vitrified sandbag back. I put it on the table in the pile for the display. Then I frowned. 'But I didn't think building fires were hot enough to melt sand.'

'Ah, but the Beryl fire was started by a limelight explosion.' Pete nodded at the box. 'Those got plenty hot, let me tell you.'

'These things explode?' Kevin asked. He took a large step away from the box at Pete's feet.

'Well, limelights were pretty unstable, but only when they were lit. Theatres had fires all the time.' Pete shrugged. 'Some people say the Beryl's fire was a curse, though. For having the Midnight Star onstage.'

Something pinged at the back of my mind. I searched through the pile of boring papers until I found the loan agreement.

'You mean this?' I handed Pete the loan papers and he flipped through them with a low soundless whistle.

'The Midnight Star.' He shook his head.

'What is it?' I blew a loose strand of hair off my face.

Pete folded back the top three pages and then handed the pack back to me, revealing a grainy black and white photograph of the largest diamond necklace I had ever seen.

CHAPTER 8

'Wow,' I said, but wow didn't even start to cover it.

The Midnight Star wasn't just a big diamond on the end of a chain. The whole necklace was a jewel-encrusted masterpiece. Five ornamental chains of silver and diamond created a sparkling crescent. There were six small diamonds embedded in the smallest link of just one of the five chains. I did a quick calculation: six diamonds per link times twenty-four links per chain times five chains equals seven hundred and twenty diamonds, and that didn't count any of the larger stones.

Darker stones – rubies or emeralds, I couldn't tell which in the black and white photo – dotted each chain, and more large diamonds hung like teardrops from the lowest strand of the necklace. At the very bottom hung the Star itself, a square diamond the size of a deck of cards, about five centimetres across set in a silver bracket with three more teardrop diamonds below.

Kevin whistled. 'And I thought the fake one I saw yesterday was impressive.'

'How did this ruin the Beryl?' I asked, trying to look away, and failing. I'm not a diamond necklace kind of girl – I'd rather have a new graphing calculator – but I had to admit I was impressed.

Pete leant back on his heels. 'Well, back in the 1920s Mr Franklin Oswald – he was the Beryl's owner – got into financial troubles. He needed a hit to save the theatre. This was right before the Great Depression and a lot of Philadelphia theatres were struggling. There was a lot of competition and with the emergence of—'

Franklin Oswald was the Beryl's owner. I made a mental note to add his journal to the display.

'So they needed a hit . . .?' I prompted. Pete's stories had a way of taking dangerous side-tracks that could wind off in the most unrelated directions.

'Oh, right, sorry.' Pete cleared his throat and reeled the story back to the point. 'Oswald used the last of his money to commission *The Curse of the Casterfields* by some hot new playwright and put on a lavish production. And then, to top it all off, he borrowed *this* to use on opening night.' He nodded towards the picture in my hand, brows furrowed like he'd told me they'd tried to use a live crocodile onstage.

'And that was bad?' Kevin asked.

'Theatre people think it's bad luck to use real jewellery onstage,' I said. Della had a pair of real diamond earrings she wore for auditions, but she'd *never* wear them in an actual show. She also wouldn't accept flowers before the curtain call. Or even look at a peacock feather. Theatre people had a superstition about practically everything. 'But you don't seriously think the Beryl is cursed, do you?'

Pete nodded, his face grave. 'On opening night, the Midnight Star was onstage and the fire started. The necklace went missing in the confusion. Oswald had to use all the money he'd raised to repay the owner. There was nothing left to restore the Beryl. Kittie Grace died and *The Curse of the Casterfields* was never performed again. If that doesn't sound like a real curse to you, I don't know what will. Franklin Oswald never recovered. He died without a penny to his name.'

'Why didn't Mr Oswald just sell the Beryl?'

'He tried, but no one wanted to buy it. And then the markets crashed and no one had the money to buy it. The Beryl stayed in the Oswald family until his grand-niece bequeathed it to the city. People said Mr Oswald got a little odd after the fire. He became fixated on finding the Star. Spent every last penny he had on trying to track it down, and then some. That's why none of this stuff got thrown away.' Pete gestured to the piles of boxes and bags and other debris behind me. 'Oswald was obsessed.'

'So what happened to it?' Kevin asked, his eyes wide with anticipation.

'No one knows – the Midnight Star was never found.'

The two of them grinned at each other and then at the mountain of boxes we had yet to search.

'Well, at least that explains why some of these boxes are full of junk,' Kevin said. 'Oswald couldn't risk throwing anything away.' He rubbed his hands together and pulled a cardboard document box from the top of the stack balanced against the back wall. He held it to his ear and shook it gently, like a kid with a birthday present.

'Wait, you don't think it's still in *here*?' I asked incredulously.

'Why not?' Kevin asked.

'No, Alice is right,' Pete said, his voice heavy. 'Mr Oswald went over the Beryl from top to bottom. He even lived here once he lost his house. If the Star was here I'm sure he would have found it.'

I remembered the mouse-infested bedding with a shudder.

Kevin just shrugged. 'Well, I'm going to pretend it's still here. It'll make cleaning this room much more exciting.'

He put the box on the table and peeled back the lid.

He looked so disappointed I almost laughed.

'More papers,' he sighed.

I expected Pete to be disappointed too, since he'd sounded pretty interested in finding the Midnight Star too.

But the papers made him just as excited. Pete moved so fast to get a look inside, Kevin practically bounced off his stomach.

Kevin stared at him, his mouth hanging open, and then he turned to me. I just shrugged. Everyone's got something they're passionate about. Me, I like numbers. Kevin liked seeing how many spitballs he could shoot at a classmate before he got sent to the principal's office. Pete liked theatre relics.

'Oh,' Pete said. Or rather, he made the shape of the word with his mouth, I think he was too excited to get the sound out.

'What?'

'It's the script, the original script. Look at it. *Oh!* Look, there are stage directions. Someone's pencilled in *stage directions.*'

He gathered up the papers in his big meaty hands as if they were rose petals. As he lifted up the last few pages, I noticed something underneath them, five large black and white photos.

'Who are they?' Kevin asked, picking up the picture on top.

Pete glanced at the photos and then back at the script, torn between which one needed more ogling.

'Whoa, get a load of this guy.'

Kevin held up a glossy 8×12 photograph. A man stared out at me with large wet eyes, his hair slicked back against his head. It was a black and white photo, so it was hard to tell, but he seemed very pale, with dark smudges around his eyes and dark lips that had just a hint of a sneer.

'That's the actor who played Matthew Strange's role. He was quite famous in the twenties,' Pete said. 'I saw his picture in the paper when I was researching the Beryl.'

'You were researching? Why?' I asked. Had Pete been researching the history of the Beryl, or the history of the Midnight Star? I felt strangely relieved that he hadn't noticed me with Franklin Oswald's journal.

Pete looked at me like I was the crazy one. 'Because it's interesting. Oh look, there's more.'

The next photo was of an actress. She was pretty in a china-doll kind of way, her eyes and lips looked almost painted on. Her hair was bobbed and the fringe cut a harsh line across her forehead. She must have stared straight into the camera lens because I could almost feel her watching me from the photo.

I shivered and pulled out the next photo quickly, covering the woman's watchful eyes. 'Who's this?' The picture was of a girl in her early teens, her long hair hanging over her shoulders in two neat tails. 'She must have had the same role as Della.'

Pete sucked in a sharp breath and froze.

'What's wrong?' I asked quickly, handing both the photos to Kevin.

'Your sister,' Pete said sheepishly. 'I got so caught up, I

forgot she sent me to get you.'

'Della did? Why?'

'She wouldn't say. She just sent me to go find you and tell you to go to her dressing room.'

'Maybe she's found a clue,' Kevin said.

I made a sharp *be quiet* gesture. I'd been serious when I told Della to keep the case a secret. I didn't want to start a riot by asking everyone about an evil ghost. But Pete didn't seem to notice.

'I'm sure she's fine. She said she would have come herself but she needed to "secure the scene".'

Kevin gave me another, very meaningful look. He was practically dancing from one foot to the other. I guess he'd had enough of the gas house for one morning.

I took the script out of Pete's hands and stacked it carefully on the table. The handwritten notes were scrawled in a tight neat hand that would probably look very impressive in a display case. 'I'm sure she's fine, but we'll go check on her just in case. Do you want to pack up that light and take it with you?'

Pete face brightened so much it practically glowed.

Kevin helped Pete get the pieces of the limelight back into the box, then held the door while Pete angled his way into the hall.

'Thanks, you guys. This is going to be such a treat,' he said, using his chin to point at the box. He sighed happily. 'I sure envy you two. Promise to let me know if you find anything special?'

'Sure,' I said.

I was pretty sure when Pete said 'anything special' he meant 'the Midnight Star'. It looked like Franklin Oswald wasn't the only one obsessed with the necklace. I wondered how many other people in the cast and crew might be secret treasure hunters too.

Once Pete was gone, I locked the gas-house door, double-checking to make sure it was secure. Then I turned to Kevin.

'Right, let's go see what my sister wants.'

CHAPTER

9

'Della?' I'd barely knocked on the door and it flew open. 'There you are,' she said, grabbing my arm and dragging me inside. 'What took you so long?'

I opened my mouth to tell Della to stop being so impatient, but when I took a closer look, I stopped.

It looked like a small tornado had touched down in the middle of the room. Small silvery shards of mirrored glass blanketed the floor like a layer of sparkling ice. The rest of the room looked untouched, but I didn't think Della would have called me just to help her clean up a broken mirror.

'What happened?' I asked.

'You tell me! I came back to get changed into my next costume and I found it like this.' Della waved her hand at the mess.

'Whoa.' Kevin stood in the doorway staring at the mess.

'Did you tick someone off or something?'

Della's face went from pale to ashen and I glared at Kevin.

'It's the ghost,' Della whispered. 'It must be angry. With me.' The panic in her voice multiplied with every word.

Normally, I'd have thought my sister was just being dramatic. But as I looked around I couldn't help but shiver. Someone had been through that room. And they'd been angry enough to make a pretty big mess.

The make-up table had been shifted to one side and put back in the wrong place. A large bottle of baby powder lay on its side, its contents dusting the floor with fine white powder. Across the room the floor was scratched where someone had dragged a metal folding chair under the air vent. I frowned and climbed on to a chair for a better look. The screws on the vent cover had been removed and put back. Bright new scratches marked the metal.

Kevin whistled.

'OK, Della, try to stay calm. Kevin, shut the door.'

Della didn't respond, she was too busy doubled over and gasping for air. I sat my sister down in one of the camping chairs and pushed her head between her knees. I wasn't sure how much of it was an act and how much of it was real, but then again, Della is a method actress, so it was basically the same either way.

It just didn't make sense. There was hardly anything in the room to start with, so what was the point of searching

71

it? Unless it was just to upset Della, or Vivian.

I remembered how Vivian had reacted to the ghost light being left off. If someone was trying to ruin the show, they were running out of time. Moving props and breaking the set hadn't worked. Maybe they were trying something more drastic. A cold spike of fear ran down my spine. If someone really wanted to ruin the show, how far would they go?

Della sniffed and took a deep shuddery breath.

'You should make her breathe into a bag,' Kevin said. He was trying to be helpful, but all he got was one of Della's dirty looks. It was one of her better ones too. I figured if she could hand out looks like that she was going to be OK, so I knelt in front of her and asked a question.

'Was the dressing room like this when you came in?'

'No,' she said. 'I came in at about eight thirty this morning, and everything was fine. And then I went and did my scenes, and when I came back here, it was like this.' She swept her arm in a wide arc, displaying the room like it was a game-show prize.

'Is anything missing?' I asked.

Della shook her head. 'Ghosts don't steal things.'

'Della, listen,' I said, crouching beside her. 'This isn't a ghost.'

She opened her mouth to protest and I held up my hand. 'It isn't. Look.'

I pointed to the fine layer of baby powder on the floor

next to the make-up table. Della followed my finger, her red eyes widening as she saw what was there. A footprint.

I waited for the meaning to sink in. It wasn't a detailed print, so it was no good for identifying the culprit, but it did prove one thing. Della sucked in her breath. 'Ghosts don't leave footprints,' she said, her voice hollow.

I nodded and tried not to look smug. Della didn't need an *I told you so.*

'Someone is actually doing all this. They're actually trying to ruin the show!' As Della spoke, her fear melted away, burnt to a crisp by the heat of her anger. Her cheeks were so red they looked like they might burst into flames. 'I understood an angry spirit. But why on earth would a person do something like this? It makes no sense.'

She stood up suddenly. The full skirt of her maid costume sent a gust of air rushing across the dressing room floor.

'Wait,' I said, but it was too late. The fine dusting of baby powder shifted and the footprint was gone. I groaned. Della had just destroyed our first real clue. Della was too upset to notice.

'Well, they're not going to get away with it.' She spun to face me. 'You are going to figure out who it is and stop them.'

Della said it like she was giving me an order. I swallowed, hard. Arguing with my sister wasn't going to bring the footprint back. Besides, the important thing was Della didn't think it was a ghost any more. And she was still counting on me to crack the case. I didn't want to think about what would happen if I let her down. Apart from the show being ruined and the Beryl turning into a multiscreen cinema, Della would think of a million ways to torture me for the rest of my life.

'Well, don't just stand there,' Della added. 'Help me clean this mess up.'

She picked up the small wastepaper basket and started carefully brushing the shards of glass off the make-up table. I grabbed a broom from the corner, one of Della's props, and started sweeping up the mess on the floor.

'Wait,' Kevin said. Della and I both turned to look at him. 'Well, didn't you want to preserve the scene of the crime, or something?'

Della snorted. I guess she didn't think the police would be interested in dressing-room vandalism. Kevin looked at me, his eyebrows raised in a question and I motioned for him to take some pictures with his phone. For some reason he was still holding the head-shots we'd just found, and he fumbled awkwardly as he tried to get his phone out of his pocket.

'Why did you bring those?' I whispered.

'I thought Della would want to see the girl who played her.'

'Ahem.' Della cleared her throat like a disappointed schoolteacher. 'If you two are finished chatting, Vivian will

74

be back any minute. And if *she* sees the dressing room like this . . .'

She let the words hang there, knowing we'd get the picture. Vivian would be hysterical. Della gave a curt nod and went back to wiping up the loose powder.

'I'll show her later,' Kevin said. He stuck the photos on the dressing table and started picking glass out of the drawers.

It took us fifteen minutes to clean up the worst of the mess. It would have taken longer – the drawers had been open when the mirror broke and there was glass everywhere – but Kevin figured out how to pull them off their runners and dump the whole mess into the bin.

Della found a large white sheet folded at the back of the room and was about to drape it over the broken mirror, but she was too late.

The door opened half a second too soon and Vivian stepped, or rather swept, into the room. Matthew Strange followed close behind her, his right arm held close to his chest in a sling.

'I can't believe you don't have ionized water here,' he said. 'It's everywhere in Hollywood. Maybe because we're more careful with our bodies out there. You should try it sometime. It will take care of that dullness in your complexion.'

Vivian froze. I could see the retort forming on her lips, but she caught sight of Della before it made it out.

'Della darling, what are you doing?'

'Vivian,' Della said. I'm so sorry. Someone's been in our dressing room. I just came back and found it like this.'

Vivian looked around, her pale face fading another two shades as she took in the damage.

Della stuck her chin out slightly, but kept her eyes and her voice level. She knew it looked bad, but she wasn't going to back down or apologize for something she didn't do. Della was tough like that.

'Oh, Della darling, not the mirror. That's such bad luck.' Vivian held one hand to her chest and shook her head.

Matthew Strange stepped into the room and whistled. Della and Vivian both shot daggers at him. Whistling in a theatre is very bad luck. But Kevin didn't notice. His eyes bulged and his mouth hung open wide enough so I could see his back teeth. He jostled me with his shoulder and nodded his head in Matthew Strange's direction. I jabbed him with my elbow and nodded sharply for him to get it together.

Matthew didn't notice Kevin gaping, or maybe he was used to being gaped at. He looked around the room and whistled again. 'What a mess. Viv, you need to get a better rider.'

Vivian's lips tightened into a thin line. 'Matthew, darling, you may be used to getting every little thing your heart desires when you're in Hollywood, but we on the legitimate stage know the meaning of sacrifice.'

Matthew looked completely startled in a *what did I do* kind of way. Vivian showed him her back, and a lot of it. The silence was palpable.

'Matthew,' I said, doing my best to sound bright and cheerful. 'This is my friend Kevin Jordan. He's a big fan.'

Kevin turned pink to the tips of his ears. 'Hi,' he said, and held out his hand and then drew it back quickly, looking at Matthew Strange's sling and turning even redder.

'Kevin!' Matthew said in his best greet-the-fans voice. 'You're the quick thinker who immobilized my shoulder yesterday. The ER doc said you prevented a lot of damage. Good thing too, I'm filming another *Agent Zero* film this summer.'

Kevin beamed and the circumference of his eyes widened by a factor of two. 'You're doing another *Agent Zero* movie? I heard rumours, but I thought it was too good to be true. Do you really do all your own stunts?'

'You bet! And thanks to you, I'll be able to keep doing them. You saved the movie!'

Matthew Strange gave Kevin his famous megawatt smile and I thought my friend was going to melt into a puddle on the floor. I started to roll my eyes, and then stopped when I remembered how I'd acted when I met my favourite physicist Ed Witten after he gave a talk on String Theory.

'So, Kevin, what are you doing at the Beryl?'

Kevin stammered, 'I'm helping Alice clean out the

storage room. For the lobby display. For the show. There's lots of stuff in there. Maybe you want to come see—'

Vivian gave a strangled cry before Kevin could finish his sentence. Horror blooming all over her face.

'It's her,' she said, pointing one long artistic finger at the photo on her dressing table. The woman with the china-doll face stared back at us. 'It's Kittie Grace!'

An electric hum filled the room, followed by a sharp hiss of static and the ping of filaments breaking as the lights in the dressing room went out.

CHAPTER

10

Someone screamed in the darkness. I was pretty sure it was Vivian. Not even Della could have hit that note. A hand grabbed at my shoulder and pushed me into Della.

'Alice,' she hissed.

'Sorry.'

Someone shoved me from the other side and I cleared my throat and spoke loudly into the darkness. 'Will everyone just stand still? The lights will come back on in a minute.'

No one listened to me, though. How could they? Vivian was having a full-blown panic attack somewhere in the darkness.

'She's here,' she wailed like a five-alarm siren. 'She's after me because I took her part. I'm sorry, Kittie.'

She started reciting the Wandering Minstrel's speech from *The Mikado*, like a priest performing an exorcism. I wasn't sure what good it would do, but maybe theatre ghosts were different to the ones you saw in movies.

The hand grabbed my shoulder again. It was Kevin, and this time he didn't let go.

'Do you think it's the ghost?' he said into my ear.

Della must have heard him because her nails started to dig into the palms of my hand.

'Shhh,' I said quickly. Vivian's panic-fire didn't need any more fuel. 'Those workmen were just putting up the new chandelier. They probably wired something wrong and blew a fuse.'

I hoped they'd fix it soon. Della's grip was like a vice. My fingers were starting to go numb, and Vivian wasn't showing any signs of calming down – if anything she was getting worse. Her wails filled the small room like a physical presence. I shuddered slightly and then stopped myself. There's no such thing as ghosts and the only thing to be really scared of was trying to move in a pitch-black room and walking into a wall.

Vivian kicked it up another octave and I cringed. Pretty soon glasses were going to start shattering.

'Oh, wow. A real live theatre ghost. This is so authentic,' Matthew Strange said, his voice filled with glee. No wonder Kevin liked him so much. They were two of a kind.

Vivian wailed louder. And louder. And then she ran out

of air. Her screams trailed off and I heard a soft thump.

'Viv?' Matthew said. 'Where'd you go?'

The light in the hall flickered back into life, flooding in through the open door and illuminating Matthew in silhouette. Vivian lay in a heap at his feet.

Matthew knelt beside her and shook her shoulder gently until her eyes fluttered open. 'Viv, you need to stop getting so worked up. You're going to hurt yourself. Life is for living. Enjoy the moment. Be in the now. In Hollywood they do a really good Zen tea. I'll call my agent and get him to send you some.'

Vivian looked like she wanted to snap at him, but she didn't. I motioned for Kevin to turn the photo over. I didn't want Vivian seeing Kittie Grace's face and kicking off all over again. Then I stepped over Della and hit the switch for the row of lights that lined what was left of the large dressing-room mirror.

Della's face had gone pale and not just for effect. She was scared. I could feel my own face heating up. I took a deep breath and turned around.

'You should take her out to get some fresh air,' I said to Matthew, tilting my head at Vivian's shaking shoulders. He nodded at me and gave Kevin a thumbs up. Kevin grinned like a seven-year-old.

'Did you see that?' he said, elbowing me in the ribs.

I ignored him.

Della looked at me. The colour was coming back to her

face now, but her eyes were still dark with worry. 'Are you sure it isn't really Kittie?' she asked. 'She died in the fire. Maybe she's upset we're reviving the show. Maybe she wants the Beryl to stay ruined. Maybe—'

'No,' I cut her off before she could go any further. Most of the time Della was pretty sensible; sure she could be a real diva, but it never got in the way of reality. But Vivian, she was another story, and her reaction had given even me the heebie-jeebies.

'But—'

'No,' I said again.

Della stuck her lip out. 'But the photo, and the lights, and all the things going wrong. Maybe she's mad that we're doing the show . . .'

'No. You saw the footprint.'

I wanted to leave it at that, but Della didn't look convinced. I sighed and sat her down on the metal folding chair in front of the mirror. I wished I'd gotten a picture of the print before it had blown away, just to remind Della we were definitely dealing with a person. Kevin stood behind her looking at the photograph.

'The lights were just a coincidence,' I said. 'How old do you think the wiring in this place is?' I shuddered.

'There's no such thing as coincidence.' Della folded her arms and stuck out her chin. But if she was ready to argue her case, I knew she must be feeling better.

'Yes there is. Coincidences happen all the time. They're

really common. The law of truly large numbers states that with a large enough sample size, any outrageous thing is likely to happen.' I hit her with the final blow. 'I can lend you a book on statistics that explains that,' I said. 'With lots and lots of numbers to back up the argument.'

Della rolled her eyes at me, a perfect arc, then she smiled.

'Look, Della,' I said. 'Someone is trying to mess with the show. But it is definitely a person, not a ghost. And when I catch the person behind all this, I'll prove it.'

Kevin and I dropped Della off in the costume workshop with Mom and took orders for lunch. Day-old subs from the 7–Eleven wasn't exactly fine dining, but like Vivian said, one had to make sacrifices for the stage.

Della didn't want to tell Mom that someone had been through her room, but it wasn't the kind of thing you could hide. At least, not after Vivian Rollins's reaction. I'd be surprised if it didn't make the first page of the arts section. I could already see Linda playing up the ghost angle to the press. People do love a ghost story.

I convinced Della to tell Mom the truth and left them talking it out.

'Oh, man,' Kevin said, shoving his hands into his pockets as we crossed the street. 'I got to talk to Matthew Strange. *And* they're making a new *Agent Zero* movie. This is the best day ever!'

I stepped wide to avoid a puddle and walked a little faster, ignoring him.

Kevin kept up easily. He puffed out a satisfied breath. 'Don't worry, I won't forget you when I'm famous.'

I snorted.

When we reached the other side of the street, Kevin held the door to the 7–Eleven open for me and grinned. The warm air inside hit me like a wall.

'So,' he said. 'Let's hear it.'

I raised an eyebrow. 'Hear what?'

'Your theory. If you don't think it's a ghost, what's going on around here?'

He grinned at me like an angel. Anyone else would have thought he was some sort of choirboy, but I knew better.

'No way,' I said, and headed to the back of the shop where they kept the sandwiches. 'I don't have enough facts yet.'

'Oh, come on, I thought we were partners. Isn't this the part where you tell me everything we know so far and I say something unrelated that cracks the case wide open.'

'You've been watching too many cop shows.'

'OK, if you don't want to tell me *your* theory. I'll tell you mine.' He wiggled his eyebrows at me and I groaned.

'Your theory is a ghost, isn't it?'

Kevin's grin widened and I let my head fall back, staring up at the tiled ceiling.

'Fine,' I said after a moment. 'I give up. You win.'

I ran through the case with Kevin, outlining the facts and what they might mean. It felt a little strange, like talking out loud in an empty house. But Kevin listened quietly and after a few minutes I almost forgot he was there.

Fact A: Props were missing and costumes broken.

Fact B: Someone had damaged the set – leading to an accident – and smashed the mirror in Della's dressing room.

Fact C: If the show fails, the Beryl is ruined.

$$A + B + C = x$$

And it was looking a lot like x = sabotage.

'Hmmm,' Kevin said thoughtfully.

'What?' I asked, waiting for him to start teasing me about the ghost. But he surprised me.

'Are you sure it's about the Beryl?' he asked.

'What do you mean?'

'Maybe they aren't trying to ruin the show,' Kevin said. 'Maybe it's about Matthew Strange. He's famous, so maybe someone is after him?'

I frowned. He had a point. Della hired me because she was worried about the Beryl, but not everyone cared about the theatre as much as she did. I should know. Matthew Strange, though, he'd been in blockbuster movies. He was the reason the Beryl's caretaker Jarvis kept the theatre locked at all times. It wouldn't explain everything, but it was still more likely than a ghost.

'That's actually not a bad theory,' I said.

'Don't look so shocked.'

Someone cleared their throat very loudly and we both jumped. I'd been so busy thinking about the case, I'd forgotten where we were.

'No loitering,' the 7–Eleven clerk said in a sour voice.

'Sorry,' I said.

'We're getting sandwiches, sir.' Kevin's face was the picture of innocence. 'It's just . . . there are so many delicious choices.'

The clerk sucked on his teeth unhappily and then turned and disappeared back towards the counter.

'Man, that guy gives me the willies,' Kevin said, dropping the angel act.

I grabbed a roast beef sub for me, veggie for my mom and tuna salad for Della and hurried towards the counter.

'So what's our next move?' Kevin asked, adding a meatball marinara to the top of the pile.

'*Our* next move?'

'Yes, *our* next move. We're a team, remember? Besides, you need someone you can trust. An outsider,' he said. 'Because unless you think a ghost is behind all the problems, the culprit is one of them.' He pointed across the street in the direction of the Beryl.

Kevin was right. I should have never let him spend so much time with my dad, he was getting way too sharp. I didn't want to believe it, but the way Jarvis guarded the building the only person who could have prised up the safe, or smashed Della's mirror, had to be someone with access to the Beryl. It had to be someone I knew.

I put the subs on the counter and ignored the suspicious look the clerk gave me when I handed him a twenty. He checked it with one of those counterfeit detector pens three times before giving me my change.

'I'd like mine hot,' Kevin told the clerk with an angelic grin.

The man took Kevin's sandwich and actually backed towards the microwave so he could keep watching us. Kevin leant against the counter as we waited.

'So,' he prompted. 'Our next move?'

I sighed. 'I'm not sure. I need time to think. We need to figure out how the facts fit together. And we need to finish cleaning out the gas house for the lobby display.'

Somewhere on the other side for the counter, the microwave dinged.

'Wait, we need to keep doing that? It's so gross in there. Isn't solving the mystery more important?' Kevin practically batted his eyelashes at me.

'Nope. Cleaning the gas house is our cover. Besides, Linda needs a display and I don't want to let her down. And don't even think about slinking off to make pie-eyes at Matthew Strange and leaving all the work to me. If you're in for the case, you're in for the cleaning.'

The clerk came back and handed Kevin his sandwich.

'Thank you, sir, I'm sure I'll enjoy it.'

'I'm sure,' the clerk sneered, and watched us like we were criminals until we left the shop.

CHAPTER

11

'We're going to have to clean that before we go home,' I said, pointing at the neon green staining the Beryl's facade. *Beware the Curse.* Kevin stopped in the middle of the street and stared at me. 'Wait, you're going to clean up after that brat?'

I shrugged. 'Someone's got to do it.'

Kevin stared at me, open-mouthed. A car honked and I grabbed his arm, pulling him on to the pavement and up the Beryl's steps.

'Besides, it's like you said. If we clean the wall, we'll have another chance to catch him when he comes back in the morning.'

Kevin's gape turned into a grin and he clapped his hands, rubbing his palms together like some sort of arch-villain.

'All right,' he said. 'Payback!'

I rolled my eyes. I didn't care about revenge, although I *did* want my phone back. More importantly, Kevin had been right when he said the graffiti wasn't normal. Now that the Beryl's equation was starting to add up to sabotage, I had to wonder if there was more to the graffiti bandit than just some bored kid looking for trouble. I needed to catch him to get some answers.

The front door to the Beryl swung open so suddenly I almost dropped the sandwiches. Jarvis, the Beryl caretaker, glared out at us. He wore black from head to toe and crêpe-soled shoes. His hair was scraped back into a ponytail and his fingernails were dirty and cracked. And he guarded the doors to the Beryl like a dog with an extra-special bone.

'Cast and crew meeting on the stage. They're waiting for you.' His voice was gruff, like he had better things to be doing than delivering messages.

He held the door until we were inside and made a show of locking it behind us. Then he stalked off without waiting to see if we would follow. I guess he assumed we would.

'Wow, I don't know who's worse, him or the Seven–Eleven guy,' Kevin said. 'What's the meeting about?'

'Probably something about the blackout,' I guessed.

My stomach growled. Kevin's meatball marinara was making my mouth water, but if Linda said everyone needed to be there, then that meant me and Kevin too. I sighed. At least I hadn't gotten a hot sandwich. Theatre meetings could take a while. Every announcement was its own three-act play. And there's nothing worse than cold marinara.

'Come on, Mom and Della are probably already there,' I added.

'Wait . . . we're going *now*?' Kevin looked at me incredulously.

'Yep.'

'How about I eat my sandwich and meet you later.'

'Nice try,' I said, linking my arm through his elbow so he couldn't get away. 'We're a team now, remember?'

Kevin and I were the last to arrive. Linda stood on the stage, her phone pressed to her ear. She was probably giving another interview. She waved us forward to where the rest of the cast and crew sat in the front rows of the audience. Mom and Della sat in the front row. Frank sat on the other side of the aisle with Matthew and Vivian. I craned my neck. Jarvis scowled at me from a few rows back. I couldn't see Pete anywhere.

I slid down the aisle and took a seat next to my sister. Kevin sat next to me, and I let him get his sub out of the bag before I passed the other two sandwiches to Mom and Della and started to unwrap mine. Della opened her eyes wide and flicked them at the brand-new theatre seat beneath me. I wrapped the sandwich back up and sat it on my lap with a sigh. Della leant over me and smacked Kevin on the arm as he took an enormous bite.

'What?' he asked, his mouth full of meatball.

'The seats,' Della hissed. Kevin looked around. Every eye in the room was on him, all of them disapproving. Maybe Della had done me a favour. Kevin's face turned about thirty per cent more red. He swallowed hard and carefully put the wrapper back on his sandwich, and then put the hot sandwich back in the brown paper bag.

'Well, that looks like everyone,' Linda said as she pocketed the phone. She looked up to the light booth. 'Pete, are you up there?'

The stage lights dimmed and brightened like the nod of a head.

Linda nodded, satisfied. She stood centre stage and brushed the dust from her hands. 'Thank you all for coming. I know this is your lunch break. I know how hard all of you are working and I just wanted to say, keep up the good work. Apologies for the lights failure earlier – we blew a fuse wiring in the gorgeous chandelier from our angel Irinke. Luckily, Pete was on hand and fixed it right away.' She applauded in the direction of the lighting booth and Pete took another virtual bow making the lights of the chandelier dance and sparkle overhead. I arched an *I told you so* eyebrow at my sister, which she expertly ignored.

Linda continued. 'I'm also pleased to report that we

have sold out for opening night.'

A small murmur of approval rose and then fell again as Linda held up her hand.

'Irinke has been spreading the word about *The Curse of the Casterfields* to all her friends, and I've been doing my part as well. Of course, we all know having the very fine Matthew Strange in the cast has helped enormously.'

Matthew held up his hands as if to protest, slipping his right hand out of the sling to do so, but he didn't seem to mind all the extra applause one bit.

'*But,*' Linda continued once Matthew had taken his second bow, 'we can't get complacent now.'

Linda droned on about the importance of the Beryl to the city and the history of the theatre. It was warm and I stifled a yawn. I started calculating the number of seats in the theatre, glancing around to see if I was the only one who was bored. I was. The rest of the cast and crew were completely absorbed in Linda's speech. And Kevin was looking across the aisle at Matthew Strange with stars in his eyes.

It was the first time I'd seen everyone who had access to the Beryl together in one place. My stomach twisted as the germ of suspicion Kevin had planted took root. The person responsible for the trouble at the Beryl was probably sitting in this very room.

'It isn't enough for us to sell out opening night,' Linda said, her eyes glowing with passion. 'We need to dazzle our audience. We need to show them the magic of the Beryl.'

I tipped my neck to the side, pretending to stretch, and tried to get a good look at everyone's face, as if their guilt might be written there. But it was no use. I was in a room full of actors. Everyone nodded and applauded in all the right places. It could be any one of them. The germ of suspicion started to multiply and I squashed it down. Guessing based on looks was sloppy. All I needed was to figure out the facts – those never lied.

Kevin nudged my shoulder and gave me a questioning look.

I shook my head. So far, no one knew I was looking into the disturbances. I didn't want to blow my cover by speculating out loud.

He nudged me again and I realized Linda was staring at me.

'Alice?'

I stood up and tried not to look startled.

'Yes?'

'I was just telling everyone about the lobby display you're working on.' She frowned at me and then turned to the rest of the group. 'If anyone has any ideas for the lobby, be sure to let Alice know. Thank you, Alice.'

I waved once and sat down, feeling my face go hot as my mom led the crowd in a round of polite applause. I've never understood how Della could enjoy people clapping for her.

'And Pete has worked wonders reproducing the original set.'

Everyone clapped again. And the lights above the stage danced through a rainbow of colours in a visual salute.

'And despite his best efforts to interfere, Rex Cragthorne has been reprimanded by the County Clerk for wasting the court's time filing frivolous injunctions.'

Injunctions? It was no secret media mogul Rex Cragthorne wanted the Beryl to fail. He'd been furious when the city decided to give Save the Beryl another chance to make the theatre a success instead of letting him turn it into a cinema complex. But this was the first time I'd heard about him taking legal action to try to stop the show. I wondered how far Cragthorne would go to get his own way.

'But,' Linda continued, raising her hands for quiet, 'we are not out of the woods yet. The Clerk won't accept any more claims from Mr Cragthorne until after the first run of the show. If we haven't proved ourselves by then, he will be free to start making complaints again. I'm sure you all understand just how important this show is. We only have four more days until opening night, and I know we can pull together and give the audience something amazing. And I want everyone to be extra-vigilant. Rex Cragthorne is a despicable man. Who knows how low he'll stoop?'

'Hear hear,' Frank shouted from his seat.

My mind drifted to Della's list of things going wrong.

Scaring the cast and crew into quitting would be one way to ruin the show.

Della elbowed me hard in the ribs. When I turned both she and Kevin were staring at me with wide eyes. I guess they had the same idea about Cragthorne as I had. I put my fingers to my lips. Dreaming up theories was easy, but even if we were right, we didn't have any proof. Besides, if Cragthorne was behind it all, that meant someone at the Beryl was working for him. If they realized anyone was suspicious of them, they might start doing a better job covering their tracks.

I mouthed the words *not here*. And Della nodded sagely.

Linda smiled down at us from the stage, coming to the grand finale of her speech.

'Remember, no matter what happens, we are a family, bound together by our love of the stage. We will never forget that one truth we all live by: The Show Must Go On!'

CHAPTER 12

We ate lunch in the workshop, everyone except for Matthew. He needed time to meditate.

Linda ordered celebratory cheesesteak sandwiches and everyone helped themselves. The hot cheese and grilled onions made my mouth water. And my roast beef sub with slightly soggy bread didn't look quite as mouth-watering as it had before. Kevin finished the last bite of his meatball marinara and helped himself to a cheesesteak as well.

'What?' he said, looking at me. 'I'm hungry.'

I looked at him hard for a moment, and then shrugged and took a cheesesteak too. Who could say no to Philly's favourite sandwich?

After lunch, Linda wanted to see what progress we'd made in the storage room, so she followed me and Kevin as we made our way back to the gas house, taking deep breaths and reminding us to smell the history. I'd smelt enough history for a lifetime – it smelt like soot.

'Ashley? What are you doing down here?' Linda asked as we came around the corner and saw Irinke's rabbit-faced nephew. 'We were just having lunch. If I'd known you were still in the building I would have come and found you.' Linda looked around quickly. 'Is Irinke here too?'

Ashley pulled his hand away from the door handle and there was something about the way he stuck his hands in his pockets that made me glad I'd locked the door. Maybe Ashley was Cragthorne's man on the inside.

'No, Auntie Irinke went with the Ziegers for lunch, but she said she wanted to see the treasures you've dug up, so I thought I might come back and investigate.' He looked around nervously, like a small child caught stealing candy.

I shook my head. Ashley's body language read guilty even when he was just standing still, but no, I didn't think he was the culprit. He was basically Irinke's shadow. If he really wanted to hurt the Beryl, all he had to do was talk her into ending her patronage.

'Well, we are very glad she's taken an interest in the Beryl. The new chandelier is stunning.'

Linda turned to look at me, opening her eyes wide to tell me to hurry up. Ashley Barscay and his aunt were minor royalty, literally, and were not to be kept waiting. I took the key from round my neck and unlocked the door, ignoring the eyes on my back.

Two steps inside the door I tugged the light cord. Everything was just the way we'd left it before we'd gone to see Della, but for some reason I couldn't shake the uneasy feeling that I was missing something.

'We haven't found much yet,' I said with an apologetic shrug. 'There's a lot to go through. But I put anything that looked interesting on the table over here.'

Linda picked her way across the room, carefully avoiding the larger dust piles and cobwebs that clung to the edges of the room. Ashley followed behind her. He looked more comfortable that way.

I showed Linda what we'd found. She wasn't that interested in the sandbag or the papers. When I told her about the limelight she perked up a little bit, but it wasn't until I showed her the costumes that she got really excited.

'Oh, these stoles are lovely, Alice. I'll get your mom to clean them right away, but this dress. Here,' she handed it to me. 'Hold it up.'

I lifted the blue ballgown I'd found by the shoulders and held it up until the hem just brushed the gas-house floor. It was decorated with rows of frothy white lace and a navy blue sash and was surprisingly heavy.

'It's perfect,' she whispered, a fanatic gleam in her eye. She looked inside the dress until she found a small silk tag that had been hand-embroidered with the words *Kittie*

Grace Act II. I could see a scheme forming as her eyes flicked over the dress.

'Take that to your mother. She's still finishing Vivian's ballgown, but using one of the original costumes would be so authentic. Virginia is going to go crazy when she sees this. Hold it up a little higher. I want to tweet this to our supporters.'

My mom would go crazy all right, she loved original costumes. But I didn't think *Vivian* would be excited at all – she was already convinced the ghost of Kittie Grace was out to get her. Before I had a chance to protest, Linda lifted her phone and snapped a picture. The flash went off, making my eyes dazzle. My face felt hot. But Linda didn't notice.

'Oh, this is so exciting.' She clapped her hands together and looked around. She looked at the boxes and licked her lips. 'Shall I open one?'

'Knock yourself out,' I said, rubbing my eyes. Small rainbow flashes danced behind my lids. I was pretty sure I could hear Kevin laughing under his breath. I scowled in his general direction. The laughter stopped.

Linda took her time choosing a box, like a kid spending their last dollar in the sweet shop. She finally decided on a small black case tucked in the corner of the room.

'Let's see what we've got.'

I crossed my arms and waited for disappointment to fill her face, but it never came. Linda gaped. Her eyes bulged behind her designer spectacles and her mouth dropped open.

'What did you find?' Kevin asked, crowding around her to get a better look.

His mouth dropped open too.

'Oh my,' Linda said. It came out in a breathless little whisper.

'Is that what I think it is?' Kevin asked.

I blinked furiously to clear my vision and hurried around to look inside the box.

It sparkled. Gems and jewels of every size, shape and colour gleamed out at me. It looked like the inside of a pirate's treasure chest. My heart rate kicked into high gear as Linda reached into the box and pulled out a large, crescent-shaped necklace of diamonds and silver. The Midnight Star.

'No way,' I said. It wasn't possible. How could it have just been sitting in a box for all those years? Franklin Oswald would have to have found it in a heartbeat. The necklace sparkled in the light of the bare bulb.

Kevin looked at the necklace and then back into the box. 'What the—' he said, reaching in with one hand and pulling out a second necklace, exactly like the first. And then a third. 'How many of these things are there?'

Ashley Barscay snatched the necklace out of his hands.

'Hey!' Kevin shouted.

I blinked. I hadn't heard Ashley move from the doorway.

He took a sheet of newsprint from the table and held it behind the necklace, peering through the enormous stone. Then he touched it to his lips.

'It's fake,' he said after a moment.

Linda turned to him without a word, unable to speak. He took the necklace from her hand and tested that one as well.

'What do you mean *fake*?' I asked.

'They're paste.' He rolled the word 'paste' out of his mouth like a rotten grape. 'Look, you can read the paper through the stone, and when you touch it to your lip it stays cold.'

I nodded slowly. Diamonds have a high refraction index: they bend light, a lot. It's what makes them sparkle, but it would also make it impossible to read anything through them – the words would be too distorted. Diamonds are also excellent heat conductors, which is why they are used in a lot of electronic equipment. A real diamond would soak up the heat from your skin and get hot right away, a fake one wouldn't. They were two quick and dirty tests, but I got the feeling Ashley knew what he was talking about. With an aunt like Irinke, he'd probably seen more real diamonds in an afternoon than I'd see in a lifetime.

Linda looked from the necklace to Ashley and then back again. 'All of them?' she asked quietly.

Ashley smiled, it was the first time I'd seen him do that.

It made him look almost normal. 'I'll check,' he said, but he didn't sound very hopeful.

There were five Midnight Stars in total and all of them were fake. So were the rest of the necklaces, bracelets, earrings and brooches in the box. They were all paste.

'Very good paste,' Ashley assured us. 'But paste nonetheless.'

'What's the point of having five fake necklaces?' Kevin asked. He glared at the box.

'They only borrowed the real necklace for opening night,' I said. 'They must have had replicas made for the rest of the performances. And it would have made sense to get more than one replica.'

Linda gave a heavy sigh and let the necklace slide through her fingers back into the box.

'I should have known it was too good to be true,' Kevin said.

'Hmm . . . maybe, but it isn't a total loss,' Linda said, drumming her fingers along her arm. I could actually see her forming a plan. 'I'd been thinking about having a silent auction during intermission on opening night. A chance for our patrons to take home a piece of Beryl history.'

'You're going to auction them off?' I asked.

'Not all of them. We'll use one in the show. Ashley, maybe your aunt would wear one to one of her parties this week. I know they aren't real diamonds, but in a way they're even better than a boring old diamond necklace bought from a store. These replicas have *history.'*

Linda was the queen of spin.

Ashley looked at Linda and then at the necklace. Something cold and calculating flashed across his eyes. I wondered if asking a Barscay to wear a paste necklace was an insult. But then he smiled and took the necklace.

'I'm sure my Aunt Irinke would be thrilled. She does so love the Beryl.'

'Alice, I want you to have one too. For the lobby display. I want it right in the centre of the room where everyone can see it. And I'll make up some little auction cards for you to put by the things we're selling.'

I could see the wheels spinning now as Linda thought of a whole new campaign strategy to fill seats and make *The Curse of the Casterfields* the biggest show Philadelphia had seen for a decade.

'Ashley, if you'd be so kind, I'd love to interview you about diamonds. For the Beryl blog. You know so much. And Alice, take that dress to your mom. She'll need to do a fitting for Vivian right away to get it ready in time for opening night.'

Linda took Ashley by the arm. He hesitated slightly, then followed her out of the room. Or he tried to. Linda stopped suddenly in the doorway.

'Alice,' she said, turning around with an apologetic smile. 'I'm sorry, it slipped my mind in the confusion, but when I was coming back from picking up lunch I noticed we'd had another visit from our artistic friend . . .'

'Don't worry,' I said, ignoring Kevin's wrinkled nose. 'Cleaning up that graffiti is next on our list.'

CHAPTER

13

It took us the rest of the afternoon to scrub the Beryl clean. Tiny flecks of neon green still stained the grout between the bricks, but without a pressure washer there was nothing I could do about that.

Kevin's phone rang. He hit 'ignore' and kept scrubbing. 'I am really looking forward to getting my hands on this kid,' he said, wiggling his pruney fingers at me. 'Do you really think he'll be back?'

I shrugged. 'It was your theory.'

Fifteen minutes later, Kevin's phone rang again and did not stop.

'Answer your phone,' I said, after he hit 'ignore' for the fifth time in a row. I peeled off my gloves and dumped the pail of dirty water into the nearest storm drain.

Kevin gave me his most innocent eyes as he followed

me down the alley to the Stage Door. We'd propped it open so we could get in and out without having to go through Jarvis. I wasn't buying it for a second.

'You're going to have to go home at some point. You can't sleep here.' I waited for the door to close behind us and gave it a gentle shove, making sure it was secure. 'You can come back and see Matthew Strange tomorrow.'

Kevin just shrugged and followed me down the hallway, through the theatre. 'Or we could stay here and have a stake-out for the graffiti artist. Or for the ghost,' he said.

'There is no ghost. I thought you agreed with me?'

'I agreed that a ghost isn't causing the problems. I didn't agree there was no ghost at all.'

I counted up in primes and resisted the urge to shove my sponge down the back of Kevin's shirt.

'Come on, it'd be awesome. If we get a recording we might be on *America's Most Haunted Cities*! They pay five hundred dollars for a video.'

I pushed through the door to the costume workshop. Della sat cross-legged on the couch, doing her breathing exercises. Mom was there too, pinning together what looked like an upside-down rose on the dressmaker's dummy. The red-orange fabric glowed like an open fire beneath the light. The dress was too modern to be a costume for the show.

'Who pays five hundred dollars for what?' Mom asked, her mouth full of pins as usual.

My stomach dropped. The last thing I needed was Mom thinking I was on some dangerous ghost hunt.

'Nothing,' I said a little too quickly.

Mom stood up straight and looked at me, hard. I sighed. I didn't want Mom to know I was on a case, but I didn't want to lie either. I settled for being vague.

'Kevin thinks if he gets a video of a ghost, some TV show will pay him for it – which is silly since there are no such things as ghosts.' I directed the last half of that sentence at Della. She paused mid-breath to roll her eyes artistically.

Mom's face softened. 'A good theatre ghost would never be caught on camera. But you are welcome to try. Perhaps you'd donate some of your winnings to the Beryl if you succeed?'

Kevin gave my mom an *aw-shucks* kind of smile. I cringed. But at least she wasn't suspicious any more. Kevin kept his angel face on until he had his back to my mom, then his grin turned devilish.

'I'll see you tomorrow.' Kevin gave me a meaningful look. 'Bright and early.'

'I'll walk you out.' Della closed her book and stood. 'You'll need Jarvis to unlock the front door.'

Della ushered Kevin out of the room and I threw him a look that said *don't give her any spooky ideas*. I'd almost convinced Della a ghost wasn't the culprit and I didn't want him undermining my logic.

'I like your friend,' Mom said after Kevin was gone.

'He's OK,' I said. 'What are you working on?'

Mom spun the dummy around. 'It's Della's dress for the opening night party. Isn't it to die for?'

I shrugged. Della could make anything look good.

'And just you wait until you see what I've designed for you!' Mom said. Her eyes glazed over and I could see her designing in her head.

I shifted uncomfortably. Dresses really aren't my style. On a Venn diagram of my style and dresses there is zero overlap. But Mom's convinced that if she designs just the right kind of dress, I'll love it.

'I found something for you, in the gas house,' I said, doing my best to change the subject. I'd picked up the ballgown again on the way to see her. I held it up as Mom refocused her eyes in my direction.

She took one look and almost dropped the pins. 'Oh my. Do you know what this is?' She stepped across the room slowly towards the dress, the way people in horror movies walk towards Dracula when he's using his hypnotic eyes. My mom isn't just a costume designer, she's a costume *fanatic*. 'Silk taffeta,' she whispered. 'And genuine hand-knotted lace. Alice, this dress is exquisite.' She ran the fabric through her fingers.

'Linda thought it might fit Vivian.'

Mom took the dress out of my hands and held it up. 'Oh, she does, does she?' The corner of her eye twitched. It wasn't a question, more like a frustrated statement. 'Producers always think fitting a costume is like trying something on at a shop.' She snorted, crossed her arms and scowled at the dress. 'But, maybe . . .'

Della came back into the dressing room. 'I'm starving.'

Mom's head snapped up and she looked at her watch. 'Well, if I start anything now it will take hours, so why don't we call it a night and go get dinner. There's an Indian restaurant around the corner, Alice. Want to come?'

My stomach growled.

Mom smiled. 'I'll take that as a yes.'

Mom was distracted all through dinner. I could practically see her redesigning the ballgown in her head, filling in the gaps and holes with clever draping and rescued lace. But she resisted the urge to pull out her notebook and start sketching right there at the table. Instead, she listened as Della told her about that day's rehearsal in exhaustive detail.

'And what about you, honey? How was your day?' Mom turned to me as Della paused for a bite of rice.

'OK, I guess,' I said, swallowing hard. I'd spent most of the day investigating Della's case, and getting frustrated by how little progress I was making. But I couldn't tell her that.

'Did anything exciting happen?' Mom leant a little further forward. If it had been Dad asking, I would have been convinced he already knew and was just working me for details. But I was pretty sure Mom was just asking because she wanted to talk.

'We found some replicas of the Midnight Star,' I said.

I told Mom all about that afternoon in the gas house and we spent the rest of dinner talking about all the fabulous fake diamonds, emeralds and pearls she'd worked with over her years as a costume designer.

'Why is it bad luck to use real jewels anyway?' I asked as the waiter dropped off the bill.

'Well, in the old days, poorer companies would try to look like they had more money by blowing all their money on real jewellery. I guess they thought if the show was a hit, they'd make the money back. But it usually didn't work. People started thinking using real jewellery led to bankruptcy and ruin.'

I rolled my eyes. 'That is some seriously faulty logic.'

'That's what superstition is,' Mom said. 'Now let me go pay and I'll take you girls home.'

Della pounced the moment Mom got up to pay the bill. 'So, what have you found out?'

'I don't know,' I said. 'I'm pretty sure someone is trying to sabotage the show, but I don't know who.'

Della rolled her eyes. 'It's obviously Rex Cragthorne. Linda said he was despicable – he would do anything to ruin us.'

'He *might* be behind it, but he isn't the one actually causing the trouble. It has to be someone with access.'

Della frowned, her lips turning down in a tight line that told me what she thought of that. 'But we're all working so hard to put on the show. I can't believe anyone at the Beryl is trying to ruin it. No one in the cast would do something so underhanded. It's Cragthorne, and he must have someone else working for him.'

Now it was my turn to scowl. 'Della, I'm telling you, the cast and crew are the only ones with access to the building. Therefore, one of the cast or crew *must* be the culprit.'

Della pushed the rice on her plate around with the edge of her fork. She'd ordered the mildest thing on the menu, but she was still sweating like she was eating straight chillies. After a heavy silence she looked up at me. 'There is one other explanation,' she said stubbornly.

I groaned. I was going to kill Kevin.

'It isn't a ghost.'

'Just consider it, Alice. What if Vivian is right? What if it is the ghost of Kittie Grace? What if we're making her angry by putting on *The Curse*?'

'Della, there's no such thing as ghosts.'

'How do you know?' she asked sharply. 'Can you prove there isn't a ghost? I mean, really prove it with evidence and everything?'

'No, but come on, Della.'

'It makes more sense than thinking one of the Save the Beryl campaigners is sneaking around trying to sabotage the show.' Della's face went stony. I could practically see her digging in her heels.

I felt awful. No one wanted to find out that people they trusted might have betrayed them. But I couldn't stop now. Until I found the culprit, everyone would be a suspect, and as much as Della said she believed in the cast and crew, she'd never be able to really trust them. Besides, if they were really desperate to sabotage the show, who knew what they might try next?

We finished our dinner in silence. Mom came back from paying and the three of us walked outside. It was snowing – fat heavy flakes that caught the lights of the street as they fluttered to the ground. The noises of the city were muffled and everything seemed cosy and calm. Well, as cosy as below-freezing temperatures can feel.

Mom dug through her purse looking for her car keys. 'Alice, I want to swing by the theatre and jot down a few ideas I had for the dress before I drive you home. Is that OK? Do you want to call your father?'

Dad was probably already gone on his undercover waiter gig, but I didn't think that was what Mom meant. She wanted me to let him know I'd be home late.

'It'll be fine as long as we don't take too long,' I said.

Mom nodded, too distracted to notice Della was giving me the silent treatment. For the first time in my life, I felt grateful for a dress.

CHAPTER 14

Mom drove slowly through the snow-filled streets. There wasn't much traffic and I could hear the car's wheels crunch against the snow. She found a parking spot just outside the Beryl in the cone of orange light under a street lamp.

'Are you coming in?' Mom asked as we climbed out of the car.

'I left my bike locked up over there. Let me put it in the car first so I can ride over in the morning.'

'You should get your father to drive you.' Mom pursed her lips and left it at that. 'I'll leave the door unlocked.'

I watched Della and Mom disappear into the darkness outside the street light and then I hunched my shoulders and walked along the street. The 7–Eleven was still open, its green neon light tinting the snow. As I peered inside I noticed the same clerk behind the counter and wondered if he worked there twenty-four hours a day. No wonder he was so cranky. The man probably needed a nap.

I unlocked my bike from the lamppost nearest the corner and shoved it back through the snow, banged off the ice clumps that had stuck in the treads and tossed it into the boot of Mom's rental car. Then I stuck my hands back in my pockets and started across the street.

Della hadn't spoken to me since we'd left the restaurant. But I was pretty sure it wasn't me she was really mad at. As much as she liked drama, I knew Della didn't really believe in ghosts.

I stepped up on to the kerb and froze.

There was a light bobbing up and down in the alley to the right of the theatre and the unmistakable sound of snow being crunched underfoot.

No one was supposed to be at the Beryl. Jarvis always locked up after everyone left. Mom and Della were there, but they'd used Mom's key and gone inside through the front. The chicken jalfrezi I'd just eaten shifted uneasily in my stomach and I swallowed hard.

I could just run up the steps and go inside where Mom had turned on the lights and it was safe. But I wouldn't be much of a detective. I took a deep breath and walked towards the alley, my heart hammering against my sternum.

It was empty.

A gust of wind kicked up a fine powdery mist of snow, making phantom shapes in the dim light. I felt a chill that had nothing to do with the cold. What if I was wrong? What if there really *was* a ghost haunting the Beryl? I took a step back, and as I did, noticed a line of footprints dimpling the snow leading into the alley. My breath whooshed out in relief and my cheeks grew hot. No ghost. Ghosts didn't leave footprints. For a minute there, I had been getting as bad as my sister.

I stared at the footprints, forcing my brain to be rational. It was still snowing, fat flakes were already start-ing to cover the trail so it must have been made recently. I followed the footsteps past the wall of the Beryl to the very end of the alley, right up the two concrete steps to the Stage Door. Cold air burnt the inside of my nose as I inhaled sharply. There were no prints leading out of the Beryl. Whoever had snuck in, was still inside.

My heart started thumping in high gear. It didn't make sense. I'd made sure the Stage Door was closed and locked myself. No one should have been able to get in that way. But when I pushed on the door, it swung inwards, opening up a rectangle of total black. I swallowed. Whoever was inside might be the person behind all the problems at the theatre. And if they could get the Stage Door open, maybe Della was right. Maybe it wasn't someone from the cast and crew. I stepped inside, stumbling over a small plank of wood that someone had shoved in the doorway to keep it from locking.

I sucked in my breath and listened. Nothing but the sound of blood rushing through my ears and a low sick feeling in the pit of my stomach. Mom and Della were probably in the costume workshop by now, I swallowed hard. Someone had to be in there, sabotaging something right now, and this was my chance to catch them in the act. A sudden dull thud and creak to my right made me jump, but I managed to keep quiet.

I moved down the hallway to the wings of the stage, one hand on the wall to keep me from running into anything. Phantom flickers and flashes danced across my vision as I strained to see in total blackness. The ghost light was off again.

Another creak, louder this time. It sounded like old nails being pulled out of older wood. The sound was coming from onstage. Pete's set. It hit me in a sudden flash. Someone was trying to destroy the set!

I moved faster now, almost yelping when the wing curtains brushed across the left side of my face. I stopped, straining my ears. From several doors away, someone started singing scales. Della. She always ran scales when she was bored.

A sharp hiss of breath being sucked through teeth came from a few metres in front of me. And then the clanging of metal. Della was going to scare the culprit away. I didn't have time to be sneaky.

I let go of the wall and stepped towards the sound. The floor beneath me changed from concrete to wood. Something gritty slid beneath my feet, making it hard to grip the floor.

'Don't move,' I said in a loud voice, reaching out my hand.

My fingers closed on thin air.

A sound. I spun round, trying to locate it as it sounded again, closer this time, and I moved a little faster. Reaching out in the darkness. A soft corner of fabric brushed across my palm and I clenched my fingers. But the fabric slipped through my hand and I heard the soft footsteps of someone running away across the stage.

I ran forward, forgetting the darkness, forgetting everything except catching whoever was creeping about in the dark.

Suddenly a force round my neck jerked me backwards and I fell, stumbling to the ground. I clawed at my neck, trying to wiggle free, but whoever was holding me was strong. They dragged me backwards along the floor of the stage. I let go of the arm and reached behind me, finding a long hank of hair. I twisted it in my fingers and pulled hard.

There was a grunt of pain, but the arm didn't let go. And then a light clicked on and I was staring into the too-blue eyes of Jarvis.

'What are you doing here?' We both spoke at the same time.

Jarvis loosened his half-nelson and I wriggled out, crawling backwards on my hands and feet until I was a good distance away. I brushed my palms against my jeans, realizing that they were covered in sand. I stood up, brushing off the backs of my legs as well.

'Mom came back to do some work on Vivian's dress,' I explained. My voice sounded croaky. 'I thought I saw a light in the alley and followed someone in here. The Stage Door was propped open.'

Jarvis shook his head, still eyeing me suspiciously. I didn't move. For all I knew, he was the one I'd been chasing. But it didn't make sense. No one was more obsessed with security at the Beryl. If the culprit was Jarvis, was that all just an act? Or was it more likely that Jarvis had stayed behind to guard the building? I ground my teeth. Either way, it was just a lot of hot air until I got some actual proof.

'It's true. Someone was messing with the set. I could hear them.' I swept my arm out, gesturing around the stage, but when my eyes caught up with my hand the set was fine.

Jarvis crossed his arms.

'I know what I heard,' I said. 'Footsteps. Running away. I almost caught the person too, but you grabbed me.'

Jarvis snorted 'You're lucky I did grab you. You were just about to go over the edge and fall into the orchestra pit. That's a nasty drop.'

He nodded towards the front of the stage and I

swallowed hard. I must have gotten turned around in the dark, like divers who go too deep and don't know if they're swimming up or down. My skin went cold at the thought. The bottom of the pit was a long way down, and the floor was hard cold concrete.

'What's going on in here?' Mom's voice rang out from the lobby door. I looked across the house and saw her silhouetted in the doorway, Della by her side.

'I found your daughter flailing about on the stage. She says she heard something.'

I groaned. Mom wasn't going to like that. I took a breath and shoved my nerves back into place and did my best to keep my voice steady.

'I'm OK, Mom.'

'Alice Lynn Jones, what were you thinking? Why on earth would you go chasing after some noises in the dark. The theatre is very dangerous. You could have been hurt.' She was down the aisle and at the foot of the stage by the end of the first sentence. 'Why wasn't the ghost light on?' she asked Jarvis sharply. And then her eyes narrowed. 'What are you still doing here?'

Jarvis narrowed his eyes right back. 'I could ask you the same thing.'

Mom looked shocked. She took a deep breath, letting the tension out of her shoulders. She rubbed the bridge of her nose. 'I'm sorry, Jarvis. I know you're just making sure the Beryl is locked down for the night. I shouldn't have come back without calling ahead.'

Jarvis looked from me to my mom and then to Della at the top of the aisle. He let out a long breath. 'Dress-rehearsal week jitters,' he sighed. 'Don't worry about it, Virginia. I'll walk you out.'

I gave the pit an extra-wide berth as Jarvis led us to the lobby. He waited for Mom and Della to get their coats back on, and then he opened the theatre door and held it for us.

'You said someone propped the Stage Door open?' he asked me in a low voice as I passed him.

I nodded, surprised. Grown-ups usually ignored me about things like that, at least grown-ups besides my dad.

'I'll check it out. If you see anything else suspicious, though, come tell me, OK? Be careful.' He waited until he got my nod before he shut the door. I heard the lock click fast on the other side.

Mom read me the riot act all the way home.

CHAPTER

15

Mom dropped me off outside the house on Passfield Avenue, then she and Della headed back to their five-star hotel. I asked Della if she wanted to stay over, but she preferred the hotel's jacuzzi bathtub and steam room to the shower at Dad's. She also liked having her own bed. I think she was still mad at me.

Mom waited until I made it through the front door and waved to her from the window and then she drove slowly away.

Dad was already gone. He'd left me a note on the counter.

Stay warm and don't wait up.

Next to the note was a fresh bag of marshmallows.

I took a shower, wrapped up in Dad's old flannel robe and made myself a cup of hot cocoa with extra marshmallows before curling up on the couch. Outside, the wind stirred up the falling snow in gusts and eddies. I could see it building up on the edge of the iron bars that protected our first-floor windows. But the storm outside only made the warm soft couch cosier and the cocoa sweeter. I snuggled down into the robe, took an extra-long sip and grabbed *Fermat's Last Theorem* off the coffee table.

I only got through three pages. I wanted to enjoy the book. I wanted to sit in the warm yellow lamplight, safe from the storm howling outside and lose myself in numbers. But I couldn't. All I could think about was the Beryl. *The Curse of the Casterfields* opened in four days, and I wasn't even close to figuring out who was behind all the disturbances.

I shook myself and went back to my book. But it was no use. Not even counting primes was going to clear my head.

I went to Dad's office and got a clean notebook and a new pen. Unlimited stationery is one of the benefits of having a journalist for a father. Then I went back to the couch and started to write down what I knew.

It hadn't started out as much. A few missing props, a curtain that kept jamming, Vivian's broken shoe. But then the safe had fallen, and someone had searched Della's dressing room, broken her mirror. It all pointed to a slow, sneaky attempt to ruin the show that was getting more bold the closer we got to opening night. And the only reason I could think of for ruining the show was to ruin the Beryl too.

I frowned. I was missing something.

Matthew Strange? Kevin had suggested that the disturbances might be about the Hollywood Star, not the Beryl. But the facts didn't add up. No one had touched his dressing room or his costumes. He'd been the one to get hurt when the safe fell, but there was no way someone could have planned that to happen. There were way too many variables.

My head ached.

Mysteries are a lot like maths. Sometimes the hardest part is figuring out what you are actually trying to solve. Once you know what question to ask, then it's just a matter of solving for x.

I ran through the list again. Something sat on the edge of my memory, just out of reach. There was something all those problems had in common. But the harder I tried to remember, the vaguer my memory got.

I closed my eyes and counted in primes, focusing on the numbers and ignoring everything else: 2, 3, 5, 7. The small numbers came easily but the higher I got, the more I needed to concentrate. When I hit 513, something clicked.

Vivian's shoe, the safe and Della's dressing table were all pieces from the original 1927 production of *The Curse*. I thought furiously, trying to remember if the other problems were connected to the original show as well.

I grabbed the wall phone and dialled.

Della answered on the fourth ring, the longest she could make me wait without ignoring my call. I guess she was still upset.

'Yes?' she asked, her voice cool.

'Can you tell me about the props that were misplaced? Were they new ones or ones Pete had salvaged from the original show?'

Della was quiet for a moment. 'They were from the original show,' she said slowly.

'All of them?'

'The decanter set, the breakfast tray, the jewellery box, the bedroom safe, the banister rail.' I could imagine her standing there ticking each item off on her fingers, and the excitement in her voice grew. 'Yes, everything we had a problem with was something original. Pete was in pieces. But what does that mean?'

I thought for a minute before answering. 'I don't know.'

Della practically growled.

'I'll talk to you tomorrow,' I said quickly, before she could start asking questions. 'Night.'

I hung up the phone on Della's protest. I needed to think.

All the parts of the show where things had gone wrong had been part of the original 1927 production. Did that mean something or was it just a coincidence?

Della would probably say it was proof that Kittie's ghost

was haunting the production, but there had to be a more rational explanation. Why would someone trying to sabotage the show only go after things from the original production? Maybe it was a coincidence? Maybe old things were easier to sabotage? Maybe I had no clue what I was thinking.

I closed my eyes and kept counting.

I woke up when an arctic blast of wind swept across the living room and Dad hunched in through the front door. I sat up, wiping the sleep from my eyes. The street outside was still dark, but the clock on the microwave in the kitchen blinked 3.58.

'Hi, Dad,' I said. My mouth tasted sour and dry.

'I thought I told you not to wait up?' Dad stomped the snow off his shoes and shook his coat free of his shoulders. He was in his tuxedo and had a plastic bag from Walgreens tucked under one arm and a large catering tray of leftover hors d'oeuvres in the other.

'I didn't. I fell asleep. How was the party?'

Dad smiled and did a little dance on the doormat.

'Did something else get stolen?'

'No,' Dad sighed. 'But I did get a chance to talk to one of the security specialists who was working the party. She found me very charming.'

I scrunched up my nose.

'Don't worry, kiddo,' Dad said. 'I think she was more

charmed by the crab puffs I kept bringing her than she was by me.' He lifted the tray in his hands slightly by way of explanation. Then he kicked off his shoes and went to the kitchen where he started making a pot of coffee.

'So did you get a scoop?' I asked as he pressed the percolate button.

Dad smiled like a cat with a key to the canary cage. 'I did indeed.' He put the hors d'oeuvres away. Slowly.

'Well?' I said. I knew it must be some scoop if Dad was giving it such a big build-up.

'The guard says that there's an agent from Interpol working the case – you know, the missing Astor jewellery.' Dad was almost giddy. 'This is off the record, of course, very hush-hush.' He wiggled his eyebrows at me and I did my best to look suitably impressed.

'And that's exciting?'

'Interpol is the international police. They'd only be called in for an international criminal. A big one.'

'So you think there's some famous international jewel thief in Philadelphia?'

Dad nodded, too excited to speak. His fingers drummed against the counter like he was already typing up his story.

'What's that?' I asked, pointing at the Walgreens bag.

'I got the photos from my bow tie camera printed. Want to check out the Liberty Ball?' Dad sat down on the couch next to me and slid the photos out of the envelope and started flipping through them.

The photos weren't going to win any awards. I got glimpses of the grand entrance to the Academy of Natural Sciences. Tables covered in tasteful white cloths and rows of silver canapé trays sat around the feet of a Tyrannosaurus rex skeleton. Most of the shots were oddly framed, cutting off the top half of faces, leaving us looking at a lot of chins. I imagined it was pretty hard to aim a bow-tie camera. It was easier to see the people in the background.

'There's Rex Cragthorne,' Dad said, holding up a photo. 'He was in an even worse mood tonight than yesterday.'

Dad handed me a photo of a man in tuxedo with a bolero tie, giant silver belt buckle and a black cowboy hat. He had a cigar clamped between his jaws so tight I could see the veins standing out on his neck. He had a mobile to one ear and an expression that said he didn't like what he was hearing.

'The city told him he couldn't file any more injunctions against the Beryl,' I said, handing the photo back.

'Did they now,' Dad mused. 'Maybe old Rexy is losing his touch. He used to have City Hall in his pocket. I wonder if someone there could give me a story.'

I flipped through a few more pictures, scanning the glamorous crowd for someone who looked like a jewel thief in disguise. I paid special attention to the catering staff. If that was how Dad was sneaking in, maybe that's how the criminal was doing it too. But no one stood out.

'Hey, look,' I said pointing to one of the shots. 'That's Irinke Barscay.'

Dad raised an eyebrow at me.

'She's the Beryl's main patron. She bought us a chandelier.'

Irinke was wearing the dress Mom had designed for her, a green sheath practically dripping with sequins and beaded fringe. Ashley was there too, looking nondescript in his tuxedo, talking to a woman in a powder-blue ballgown.

'That's her nephew.' I pointed. 'Ashley.'

Dad grabbed the photo and stared. 'You know that guy? He's talking with Connie Astor – the lady in blue. She's the one who had her sapphire necklace stolen.' Dad looked at me, his eyes gleaming. 'Do you think he'd give me a story?'

The coffee maker beeped and he bounced up to get a cup.

'Maybe, if his aunt gives him permission.'

Dad harrumphed and held up the pot. 'Do you want a cup?'

I shook my head. Dad might want to stay up and type out his notes or research international jewel thieves, but I was planning on going back to bed. 'I'll ask Ashley if he'll talk to you,' I said with a yawn. 'But I doubt he could help – I don't think he's that observant.'

Dad dumped five teaspoons of sugar into his coffee, then grabbed a water bottle from the fridge, getting ready for an early morning writing marathon. 'Well, ask him for me, you never know where a lead might be hiding.' He gave me a kiss on the forehead and then disappeared into his office.

I stood up slowly. My notebook had fallen to the floor when I'd nodded off. I reached down and closed the book, leaving it on top of my copy of *Fermat's Last Theorem*. Then I trudged up the stairs and went to bed.

CHAPTER

16

I overslept and woke up with bleary eyes in a too-bright room and the taste of stale cocoa clinging to my teeth. It was almost eight thirty. I groaned. It was too late to try to catch the graffiti bandit in the act. I rolled out of bed, hopping into clothes as I made my way across the hall to brush my teeth. A mumbled protest came from Dad's bedroom when I closed the door a bit too loudly. Then he went back to sleep and the house went quiet.

I drank a cup of coffee warmed up in the microwave and had five mini-cheesesteaks from Dad's party tray before throwing on my coat and rushing out the door. Rush hour and icy roads slowed me down even more and it was after nine by the time I wheeled up outside the Beryl and locked my bike to the lamppost outside the 7–Eleven. The clerk saw me through the window and I met his suspicious scowl with a friendly wave. Then I turned my back on him and started across the street.

I grimaced. We'd been right about one thing – the graffiti bandit had returned. The Beryl's facade had been adorned with his trademark scrawl in eye-popping magenta. This time he'd sprayed the words *Death Trap* again and again across the walls.

I ground my teeth. If I hadn't overslept, I might have caught him before he made such a mess. Now I'd have to spend all morning cleaning. I stopped mid-thought. There, standing at the far edge of the building, was Kevin Jordan. Yellow gloves on his hands, a bucket at his feet, scrubbing off the paint in slow steady strokes.

'What are you doing?' I puffed as I clambered over the snowbank on to the kerb.

'Hey, Alice.' He turned to me and smiled. It actually looked like he was enjoying himself. 'You weren't here so I couldn't do anything in the storage room. And Matthew needed to rehearse. So I got that creepy caretaker to let me in to get the bucket so I could clean this off.'

'You convinced Jarvis to let you in?' I asked.

'Hey, I'm a very convincing guy.'

I smiled, I couldn't help myself. Kevin really could sweet-talk anyone. He threw me a spare pair of gloves and an extra brush. 'Chop chop.'

Kevin and I spent the next hour cleaning. Magenta was a lot easier to remove than blue or green, and we finished before ten.

'What?' Kevin asked as he emptied the bucket into the storm drain, staining the snow on the street.

'I guess you overslept too?'

'I must have missed him by minutes. The paint was still wet when I got here.' Kevin held out the empty bucket and I dropped in my sponge. 'We'll get him tomorrow.'

'You think he'll be back? Again?'

'The wall's clean, isn't it?'

I banged on the Beryl's door and waited until Jarvis let us in. He eyed me and then Kevin and then checked the street to make sure we hadn't been followed. I wouldn't have believed it possible, but after last night Jarvis seemed even more paranoid than usual.

He let us in eventually and I started to take off my coat, then I stopped. It was freezing.

'Why's it so cold in here,' I asked.

'Heater's busted,' Jarvis grunted.

'You don't think someone—'

He cut me off. 'Naw, it's just on the same circuit as the chandelier. No one noticed that the boiler went off when the fuse blew yesterday and so it got cold overnight. I relit the pilot light, and it'll just take a while to warm back up. Till then, you probably want to keep your coats on.'

'No kidding,' Kevin said, teeth chattering.

I glanced across the room to the coatrack. It was empty except for one parka with a fur-lined hood. For a moment,

I wondered who would be crazy enough to be running around without their coat. And then it hit me.

'What are you doing?' Kevin asked as I ran across the lobby. Irinke's friend the jeweller had come through and the room was full of empty glass display cases. I dodged and weaved through the chaos until I got to the coatrack.

'That coat. I pulled it off that graffiti bandit the first time I almost caught him.'

I grabbed the coat down from the hanger and rifled through the pockets, laying the contents on the ticket counter. I brought out a fistful of paper, receipts, sweet wrappers, little balls of lint. I reached into the last pocket, a small zippered number on the inside of the jacket. My fingers closed against a small smooth block of heavy plastic. I pulled a phone out of the inner pocket. For a moment, I just stared at it. Then I smiled.

It wasn't a new phone; the screen was scuffed and scratched and a small chip of the case was missing. The back had been personalized, and the style was unmistakable. Splatters of day-glo orange and yellow fought for attention with hot pink behind a single word in midnight blue.

Benji.

The graffiti bandit's name was Benji.

A small laugh bubbled inside my chest. The phone had been there the whole time. Normally, checking the pockets would have been my first move, but I'd gotten so caught up in Della's case and the drama at the Beryl that I forgot.

I shook my head ruefully, but there was no use worrying about it now.

I flipped open the phone. Benji had been making a call every morning just before 7 a.m. Right after he'd tagged the Beryl. All the calls were to the same number. I hit 'redial' and held the phone to my ear.

A bright professional voice answered on the second ring. 'Kingdom Cinema's Corporate Office, how may I direct your call?'

Kingdom Cinemas was Rex Cragthorne's company.

I hung up quickly, my eyes wide.

'What is it?' Kevin asked.

'Benji was in touch with Rex Cragthorne.'

We stared at each other as the meaning sank in.

'Do you think he's paying Benji to spray the building, to make it look bad?' Kevin asked.

'I don't know. But now we *really* need to talk to him.'

I scrolled through the contact list until I found an entry labelled *Home*. I smiled, I couldn't help it. Benji didn't just have his home phone number saved in his phone. His address was there too.

'What's that?' Kevin asked, peering over my shoulder.

'The graffiti bandit's home address.' My smile grew a little more wicked. 'Let's go take Benji his coat back.'

Benji's house was all the way out in North Philadelphia and it took us almost half an hour to get there. As we pedalled up Route 611, the houses got older and older, the wooden porches went from straight to sagging and the ratio of windows-made-of-glass to windows-boarded-up-with-plywood shrank considerably.

We pulled up outside number 307. Once upon a time it had been the height of suburban sophistication, but that time was probably the late 1800s. There were hints of the old style, but the gingerbread shingling was filled with gaps like a row of rotten teeth. The house next door looked abandoned.

I started to lock my bike to the front porch, but the wood felt like it would give way with a sharp kick, so I locked it to the stop sign on the corner instead. Kevin pushed his bike next to mine, and I wrapped the chain around them both. Then I grabbed Benji's coat and phone and started up the steps.

A flash of magenta caught my eye and I stopped with my foot in mid-air. Kevin ran into the back of me and I stumbled forward slightly. The snow had been packed into ice on the pavement and it took me a second to get my feet back under me.

'Why'd you stop?'

I pointed to the magenta stain in the snow, and the trail of size nine footprints leading up the steps to the abandoned house. Number 305.

Before I could tell Kevin we should check it out, the plywood over the far window slid to one side and a small figure in an oversized jacket clambered over the ledge. I grabbed Kevin's arm to keep him quiet, but I was too slow.

'Hey!' Kevin shouted.

Benji froze, but only for a fraction of a second. I could see the questions gathering behind his eyes, but his instincts told him to run. He swung back through the window, sliding the plywood shut behind him.

Kevin was on to the porch in two steps and I was right behind him.

'Wait!' I yelled. There was no reason to chase the kid, we knew where he lived. But Kevin's a lot faster than I am. He made it to the window in five steps, pushed the board open and slid through the gap headfirst.

I paused at the open window. My eyes were used to the sun glaring off the snow and all I could see on the other side of the window was greenish murk.

I heard Kevin trip over something and let out a shout. I sighed and then I slid in through the window after him.

CHAPTER 17

The room on the other side of the window was cold, dark and dry. There was no furniture or carpet to absorb the sound and my footsteps echoed against the bare wooden floorboards.

'Kevin?' I said.

'Shhh . . .' he hissed from somewhere to my right. I looked, and slowly his shape started to melt out of the shadows as my eyes adjusted to the light.

'It's not like we're going to be able to sneak up on him,' I said. 'He saw us in the street.'

Kevin was quiet for a minute. I could almost feel him blushing.

'I heard him go upstairs,' he whispered. 'Come on.'

I followed Kevin up the stairs, keeping close to the wall just in case there were any rotten boards ahead. There was more light at the top of the stairs. The windows weren't boarded here and still had their glass. But snow from the storm covered the bottom half of each pane, making the light cool and diffuse. I blinked. The walls were covered in graffiti. Letters, shapes and pictures in all the colours of the rainbow chased each other along the walls. I recognized the style from the Beryl immediately.

'I think we found his lair,' Kevin whispered.

I stifled a snort. What kind of a ten-year-old has a lair? And then I looked down the hall and got my answer. The kind of kid who spray-paints an entire door black and then writes KEEP OUT in giant red letters.

Kevin took one look at the door and his face split into a wolfish grin. I could almost see him thinking, *I've got you now.*

Kevin was down the hall with his hand on the doorknob before I could blink. I looked at the door. Why bother to write KEEP OUT on it? If anything, it made the 'lair' even more obvious. It was almost like Benji wanted us to go that way.

'Wait!' I yelled, but it was too late.

Kevin grabbed the knob and pulled, yanking the door open wide and charging through the doorway right into an explosion of sparkling gold paint.

I rushed forward, my heart thumping in my chest. I kept close to the wall, out of the line of fire, and peered around the door frame just in time to see Benji's size nine boots disappear out the first-storey window. I swallowed the urge to give chase. Benji was on his home turf here. He probably had dozens of hiding places.

Behind me, Kevin was stumbling around the hallway, bumping against the walls leaving gold body prints on whatever he touched. He coughed a few times, but he didn't sound like he'd breathed in too much of the paint. He was swearing too hard to be in serious trouble.

I raised my eyebrows.

'You OK?' I asked as Kevin caught his breath and down-graded his language to PG.

Kevin wiped the back of his arm across his eyes and blinked at me. Every centimetre of the front half of his body had been gilded, even his eyelashes. He looked like the golden cherub ornament on our Christmas tree. All that was missing was the harp. Kevin flicked the paint off his fingers and looked down at his jacket.

'I'm going to kill that kid,' he said.

I shrugged. 'I tried to warn you.' And then I stepped up to the door.

It took me a minute to find Benji's booby trap. It looked like something he'd built in design and technology class. A wooden box just the right size for three cans of spray paint, three holes cut into the front so the paint could spray whoever walked through the door. The lid was loose, and when I pulled it out, I saw three drawing pins lined up with the nozzle of each can. When the door opened, the lid snapped down and the drawing pins pressed down to let the paint fly. It wasn't going to stop an intruder entirely, but it was perfect for giving Benji time to make his escape.

I looked out the now-open window and saw the track Benji's body had made as it slid down the roof of the porch and the footsteps leading to the street. I sighed, and then I had another idea.

He'd had less than five minutes to set the trap and get out the window. I got out Benji's phone and dialled my own number, and the duffel bag behind the door started ringing.

I was across the room in seconds and unzipped the bag. It was full of every colour can of spray paint in the rainbow, and then some. I pushed the cans aside and they rattled and clinked against each other, and then there it was: my phone.

I snatched it up with a small grateful sigh. And flicked through it quickly. Everything seemed fine. And there was even a video of Benji spray-painting the Beryl. He hadn't erased it. I let me smile grow a little wider. I guess he didn't think I'd find him.

There wasn't much battery left, but I used some of it taking pictures of the inside of Benji's lair. And his duffel bag full of spray paint. And his booby trap. I also copied Benji's contact list, and his recent calls list. When I was satisfied I'd collected enough evidence, I put my phone carefully back in my pocket and turned to Kevin.

'Come on, let's go give Benji his coat back.'

Kevin stared at me. 'Are you kidding? He just ran. He's not going to be waiting for us at home.'

'No, but his parents might.'

I found a rag and helped Kevin wipe off the worst of the paint and tried not to laugh. He'd need a good hour under the hot tap with a scrubbing brush and a bucket of soap to get really clean. When I'd finished, Kevin still sparkled, but it was a lot more subtle. Then we made our way out of 305 and up the steps to 307.

I brought up my fist to knock and then noticed the look of glee in Kevin's eyes.

'What are you smirking for?' I asked.

'What do you mean?' He looked shocked. 'We're gonna drop him in it, right? I'm imagining him getting walloped back to the Stone Age.'

I put my hand down. Part of me agreed with Kevin. But I knew it would be a lot easier to figure out why Benji was spray-painting the Beryl if he wasn't grounded for life. Besides, if I told on him now, I wouldn't be able to threaten to do it later.

'What?' Kevin asked, his voice moving down the scale from confused to suspicious.

'Benji will never talk if we don't have any leverage.'

Kevin stared at me blankly.

'Once we spill the beans, that's it. That's the worst we

can do. There's no way he'll tell me about why he's been spray-painting the Beryl then.'

Kevin opened his mouth, I could see the words *so what* forming and I held up my hand to cut him off.

'Just let me do the talking.'

Kevin grumbled, but nodded his head.

The door opened on my third knock. A middle-aged woman in jeans and a hand-knitted sweater opened the door. She was holding a two-year-old girl. The girl and the sweater wore matching sticky orange stains.

'I'm sorry to bother you. My name's Alice Jones,' I said in my most polite voice. Kevin's eyes popped open in mock surprise, but I ignored him.

'What do you want?' Somewhere in the background another child wailed and the woman threw an annoyed look over her shoulder.

'Nothing,' I said. 'But I found these and I wanted to return them.' I held up the coat and phone like exhibits in a courtroom.

'Is that Jamie's phone? I didn't know that was missing too.'

Jamie must have been Benji's real name. I shrugged and feigned ignorance.

'Well, thank you. Jamie isn't home right now . . .'

Kevin snorted. 'We know.' I stepped on his foot, but it was too late. Benji's mom had noticed him. Her voice trailed off and she stared at the golden angel on her front porch.

'What on earth?' she asked, her eyes narrowing.

I interrupted her train of thought before she could jump to any conclusions. 'Sorry, we just came from some community service work cleaning up graffiti.'

'Uh-huh,' she said. 'Where did you say you found Jamie's coat?'

I swallowed. I didn't want to tell her what Benji had been up to. I needed to keep that card in my pocket. But from the way she was looking at Kevin, I got the feeling she knew all about her son's extracurricular activities. And she didn't approve.

'Near the Beryl Theatre.' It wasn't a lie, not technically.

She blinked. 'That old place?'

'Anyway,' I said quickly, putting the coat into her free hand and dropping Benji's phone into his pocket. 'We need to go. It was nice to meet you.'

I grabbed Kevin's arm and hauled him down the steps.

I could feel Benji's mom watching us, but I didn't look back and after a moment the door slammed shut.

Kevin exploded. 'What was the point of that?' he asked. 'You just brought the brat back his coat. And his phone. I thought we were coming here for payback?'

I unlocked the bikes and threw my leg over the side before getting out my phone. It was good to have it back.

'Payback is useless,' I said. Benji's number was saved as an incoming call and I smiled wickedly. 'What I want are answers.'

I typed a short sharp shock of a message.

STOP SPRAYING THE BERYL AND ANSWER
MY QUESTIONS OR ELSE I'LL TELL YOUR
MOM EVERYTHING.

I attached the video of Benji in action and pressed
'send'.

CHAPTER

18

It was mid-morning by the time we got back to the Beryl. The clouds from last night's snowstorm were gone and the sun bouncing off the fresh snow dazzled my eyes. Red foil hearts and cartoon cupids decorated almost every shop window we passed.

'You doing anything for Valentine's Day?' Kevin asked, jerking his head towards the display of heart-shaped soft pretzels in the window of the 7–Eleven.

'I'm going to see my sister in a show.'

'Got a date?'

'My dad.'

Kevin snorted.

I didn't get the big deal about Valentine's Day, but I did like the box of chocolates Dad always got me. He sent one to Della too.

'Hey, look, there's Matthew Strange!' Kevin said, pointing at a man on the other side of the street. He wore a navy blue baseball cap pulled low over his face, a pair of sunglasses and a scarf. 'Let's go say hi.'

I squinted at the figure. 'How do you recognize him? You can't even see his face.' I thought for a moment. And where had his sling gone?

Kevin grabbed my arm and started pulling me across the street. 'I don't know. I can just tell it's him. Maybe it's his walk? I brought my copy of *Zero Tolerance* today. Do you think he'll sign it?'

'Sure,' I said, slowing my steps along with my words.

Matthew Strange didn't go up the steps to the Beryl. Instead, he kept walking and turned down the alley that led to the Stage Door.

'What's he doing?' I asked. 'Why isn't he going in the front?'

Kevin shrugged. 'I don't know, maybe he doesn't want to wait for Captain Creepy to open the door. Come on.'

'Wait.' I grabbed Kevin's sleeve. 'Don't you think it's a little suspicious?'

Kevin shook his arm free. 'Don't tell me you think Matthew Strange is behind all the stuff going wrong?'

I shrugged. I didn't think the movie star was, but I didn't have any proof that he wasn't either. And until I knew who was causing the problems, everyone was a suspect. Kevin looked at me the way he did when I told him I liked factoring quadratic equations.

'That's ridiculous. He's way more likely to be the victim. He came all the way from Hollywood to be in this show, and he's the only reason people are coming to see it. If he wanted to make trouble, he could just quit. Especially after that safe fell on him.'

I didn't say anything. Kevin had a point, but I didn't like the idea of leaving Matthew out as a suspect just because he was famous. That's not how a good detective works.

Kevin turned the corner. 'Great, now we missed him.'

I looked into the alley. It was empty. 'Where'd he go?'

'Into the theatre. Obviously.'

Kevin stood in the mouth of the alley with crossed arms, watching as I tried the Stage Door.

'It's locked,' I said, walking back to where Kevin was waiting.

'He probably propped it open while he ran out to get a snack.'

I snorted. Matthew Strange liked to pretend he was just a normal guy, but he hadn't gotten so much as a drink of water for himself since he'd arrived. And I was starting to suspect he hadn't really needed that sling all along, he just liked the attention.

'Whatever,' Kevin said. 'It isn't him.' And he stormed round the corner and up the steps of the Beryl, banging on the door without waiting for me to catch up.

We walked into the middle of a meltdown.

'I won't wear it. I won't!' Vivian Rollins's voice rolled out through the lobby, sending fear, determination and a hint of hysteria ringing down the hall.

I edged through the door slowly and stuck close to the wall, ready to duck and cover if Vivian decided she needed to throw something to really make her point. Kevin kept behind me.

'But, Vivian, think of the press. The original ballgown from the original production of *The Curse of the Casterfields*,' Linda said, pleading.

'I won't! Kittie Grace is already angry enough that I've taken her role. What will happen if I take her dress too? She's already tried to kill me once . . .'

I slid sideways into the room. Vivian had her back to the door, her shoulders stiff and arms held rigidly against her sides. Mom stood across from her, the ballgown I'd found in the gas house hung over her arm.

She'd been busy. The dusty blue fabric had been sponged clean. And the metres of lace trim had been carefully removed so she could reattach it after the alterations were finished. She had dark smudges under her eyes, but she didn't look tired. Mom's eyes sparkled, reflecting the blue of the dress.

Linda stood next to Vivian, her thumbs flying across her phone. She was probably writing up a new blog post about the fitting. Her face was smooth and expressionless, but her voice gave away her frustration.

'Vivian, we've been over this,' Linda said soothingly. 'I'm sure Miss Grace would understand.'

Vivian didn't budge.

'Look, Vivian,' Mom said. 'I need to take the whole dress apart and replace all the bits with holes. It will be like a brand-new dress when I'm done.' Linda looked aghast, and Mom added quickly, 'It will look just like the original, but there are too many holes to reuse all of the same fabric, and unless Vivian wants to wear a corset, there's no way she'd fit into it anyway.' Mom turned to Vivian. 'Just come with me and try it on so I can see what needs to be altered and then you can take it right back off.'

Linda turned back to Vivian. 'She's right. The show must go on, and so must the dress.'

Vivian sighed so dramatically I worried she might deflate. She looked at us each in turn, her lip trembling just enough so we could see it. 'I'll do it. I'll do it for the good of the show.' She gave a brave little sniff, and let Mom lead her away.

'Wow.' Kevin shook his head. 'She really thinks the ghost is coming to get her.'

'Seems like it,' I said. Part of me wanted to think Vivian was just pretending, for attention. I'd thought so at first, but the more things that went wrong, the more frantic Vivian became. If we didn't figure out what was going on soon, she might have a full-scale breakdown.

Linda finished typing and looked up. 'Ah, Alice, I'm glad you're here. I really need you and your friend to come through with this lobby display. We've sold out opening night, but we need everyone who comes to the show to be so impressed with the Beryl that they tell all their friends. I want people taking pictures and posting them online, real buzz creation.' She looked at us expectantly.

I waited for a second to answer, expecting Kevin to get there first. But he didn't.

'I'll do my best,' I said, feeling more than a little lame.

Linda's phone rang. 'What? Oh no, how awful, well of course I understand, if you're not well. Are you sure you don't want to keep your tickets? You still have three days to get better.'

Linda waved at us and disappeared through the lobby doors, still talking.

Kevin and I spent the rest of the morning hauling the most interesting pieces from the collection of Franklin Oswald to the lobby, sponging off the worst of the dust and laying them out in the glass display cases Irinke's friend had sent. I had to admit, a glass case made a lot of difference. In the gas house the original script looked like an old pile of papers, but lying on top of the black velvet table underneath a layer of glass it looked like it belonged in a museum.

Pete stopped by a little after one o'clock with the rebuilt

limelight and some black posterboard to mount the photos of the original cast.

I found a small pedestal case and moved it to the back wall of the room, between the two doors to the theatre, and put the vitrified sandbag inside next to an article about the fire that had destroyed the Beryl and a small card where I'd explained how sand turned into glass. Kevin looked over my shoulder and wrinkled his nose.

'What?' I asked.

'It looks like a science fair project,' he said.

'What's wrong with that? I like the science fair.'

'Whatever you say.' Kevin shrugged and I had the annoying feeling that he was letting me win the argument.

'Look, Kevin, I'm sorry about suspecting Matthew Strange. But I can't rule him out just because he's a star. I can't rule anyone out.'

'Not even Della? Or your mom?'

I let out a rough breath. 'Technically? I can rule out Della because she's the one who hired me. But my mom?' I thought for a moment, trying to think of a rock-solid reason I knew it wasn't her, beside the fact that she was my mother. 'No.'

Kevin shook his head, then laughed. 'Well, I guess if you suspect even your mom, I can't be too upset,' he said grudgingly. 'I'm starving. Come on, let's go get some lunch.'

CHAPTER 19

When we got back, we walked into the second crisis of the day.

Linda paced the lobby, bent over slightly with her ear pressed to her phone. Every now and again she broke her silence with a calm murmur of understanding. Her voice never betrayed the agitation of her feet and I assumed she was speaking to either a donor or a ticket holder, trying to reassure them.

Mom was there too. She stood behind the ticket counter furiously flipping through the large black ledger of the tickets sold.

Linda hung up the phone and started dialling the next number without looking up. 'That's fifteen people who've heard this scary rumour. Virginia, I swear I am going to take Rex Cragthorne by the neck and shake him until his teeth fall out. What's the next number?'

Mom read out seven digits and a name and Linda dialled, punching the buttons so hard I was worried she'd crack the screen.

'What happened?' I whispered to Jarvis.

'People started calling up to cancel their tickets and wanting their money back. There's a rumour going around that the building isn't safe.'

'And Linda thinks Rex Cragthorne started it.'

Jarvis nodded and rubbed his gnarled hand over the back of his neck.

I flashed back to the words Benji had scrawled across the Beryl that morning: *Death Trap*. I guess Rex Cragthorne figured if he couldn't get the courts to shut the Beryl down he'd just scare everyone away instead. I ground my teeth.

Linda finished her next conversation and hung up with a strangled sound. She was next to the ticket window and I half expected her to kick the wall in frustration. Instead, she smoothed her hand over her hair and tucked a stray hair back into place.

'Virginia, I need you to take over calling everyone who's bought tickets and assure them that the Beryl is perfectly safe.' She handed Mom the phone, grabbed her coat from the coatrack and tugged it on. 'I'm going to call in some favours with the press and get this fire put out. And when I get back, I need to talk to Alice about this lobby display. Honestly, Virginia, I thought you said she'd do a good job.'

Linda spun around and stopped cold when she saw me standing next to Jarvis.

'Linda!' Mom said sharply.

I felt like I'd been kicked.

Next to me I could feel Kevin bristling, but he kept quiet.

Linda sighed – a great big heave of a breath – and put her head in her palms. She took a breath in and looked up.

'I'm sorry, Alice. I know you worked hard on this, but the display was supposed to be something sensational.'

I didn't say anything. I looked around the lobby. I didn't know what she expected me to do. It wasn't like there had been a lot to work with in the gas house. My palms started to sweat.

Linda took another deep breath. 'I was going to talk to you. To help you, but now I need to go deal with Rex Cragthorne.' She looked guiltily at my mom and then back at me. 'I shouldn't have taken my frustration out on you. I just . . .' Her voice sounded hopeless.

I looked at Linda and I could feel my heart breaking a bit. I might not have loved the Beryl the way she did, but I knew what it felt like to have someone stomp all over your dreams. It felt rotten. I didn't want Mom to get upset, but I'd never be able to live with myself if I didn't tell Linda about Benji.

'If you could prove Mr Cragthorne was trying to sabotage the Beryl, would that help?'

Linda looked at me sharply. 'What kind of proof?'

'Like if I found someone who he paid to vandalize the front of the building.'

I could feel Mom's eyes digging into the side of my head without looking. I winced. Linda didn't seem to notice. Her face smoothed and she stood up a bit straighter. A small smile tugged at the corner of her mouth.

'If I could get someone to testify that Mr Cragthorne paid them to do it, I could take him to court. I might be able to get them to bar him from buying the building even if we did have to sell it.' The wheels in her head spun at lightning speed. 'Did you find the person spray-painting the building? Did he confess to Cragthorne paying him?' she asked.

My stomach flipped. 'Not yet, but I think he will soon.'

Linda nodded. 'OK, get the confession and bring it to me. Or better yet, bring him to me in person. Until then, I need to get this situation under control. And about the display—'

I opened my mouth, but Kevin stepped in front of me before I could put my foot in it.

'I'll help her jazz it up,' he said with a winning smile. The gold glitter might have confused Benji's mom, but it worked for Linda. She looked Kevin up and down, gave a satisfied nod and stepped towards the door. Jarvis opened it without missing a beat and Linda swept out of the theatre.

Mom stared at me. I swallowed hard. Her heels clicked as she came around the ticket counter.

'Kevin,' she said in a deadly calm voice. 'Can you give us a minute?'

Kevin looked at me and then at my mom. 'Uh, yeah, I needed to use the bathroom anyway.'

I was surprised he didn't trip over his own feet he moved so fast, scooting past us and into the theatre. He didn't even stop to take his coat off. Jarvis took one look at Mom and followed on Kevin's heels.

Mom waited until they were gone, then she turned to me. 'Alice, do you want to tell me what's going on?'

I didn't. But it wasn't a question.

'A-lice?' Mom drew out my name into two syllables. Which meant I was in two times as much trouble if I didn't start talking. I sighed.

'I figured out who's been spray-painting the front of the building. Rex Cragthorne's been paying him to do it.'

'And how did you figure this out?'

'I might have looked through his phone and found his address.' I swallowed. 'And gone over there . . .'

'Alice!' Mom looked horrified. 'Running around the city after criminals is dangerous. You're just a girl. You can't take on the world.'

'I'm not stupid. I know that. I was tailing a ten-year-old kid, not an escaped convict.'

'When I asked for your help at the Beryl, this isn't what I wanted.'

Maybe I was still raw from Linda hating the lobby

display. Maybe it was the case going in circles or the fact that I'd been stuck dealing with high-strung actors, a filthy room full of junk and an imaginary haunting instead of being at home reading *Fermat's Last Theorem*. Maybe all the spray paint I'd been scrubbing had scrambled my brain, but whatever the reason, I saw red.

'No,' I snapped. 'You just wanted me to be Della's understudy.'

Mom crossed her arms. 'Honey, if you wanted the role, you should have auditioned for it, but your sister has a lot more experience.'

I could have screamed.

'I don't want Della's part. I don't want *any* part. I keep telling you I don't like acting, but you never listen. I'm not like you. I hate being onstage. I hate wearing your stupid dresses. I don't care if the Beryl becomes a Cineplex. I like staying at home, and maths, and figuring things out. I like being a detective. And I'm good at it. If you'd just let me finish—'

'Alice Lynn Jones, that is enough!' Mom snapped, holding up both of her hands in the air. 'I forbid you from doing any more detective work. Do you understand?'

I glared at her, tears stinging my eyes. I refused to let them fall.

Kevin must have snuck out the Stage Door because he was already standing next to my bike when I got outside.

I unlocked it without saying a word. I didn't think I'd be able to, not without my voice cracking and giving me away.

I started pedalling home, hard and fast until my lungs burnt and I was sweating inside my duffel coat. Kevin kept up easily. We cycled through Old City in silence. When we got to South Street I had to slow down. My thighs didn't give me a choice.

'So, did you get grounded or what?' Kevin grinned at me.

'I don't want to talk about it.'

'What? It's no biggie. I get grounded all the time.'

I rolled my eyes, but smiled in spite of myself. 'Mom doesn't want me "playing detective",' I said.

'So don't play.' Kevin's smile spread and he sped ahead of me.

I pedalled a little bit faster, until the wind was strong enough to push back my hood. I breathed deeply as its cool fingers swept through my hair. Kevin slowed down as we turned on to Passfield Avenue and I caught up with him outside of my house.

'So I was thinking,' he said. 'About the lobby display.'

I groaned.

'You should make it about the missing necklace.'

'Why? What's that got to do with the Beryl?'

'Wow, you are the most literal person I know. It went missing there. And caused the curse. Come on, massive diamonds are exciting. Ask your dad. People like sparkly things. All you have to do is rearrange things a little and make some fancy posters.'

I leant my weight on one leg, holding the bike upright with my hip while I dug out my house key.

'You could even make it a mystery. Give people the clues and see if they can figure out what happened to the necklace.'

I scoffed. 'That's easy. It got grabbed in the panic during the fire and someone cut it up and sold it off.'

'Maybe you're right,' Kevin smirked. 'But can you prove it?' And with that he hopped down the steps and climbed on to his bike.

His words sank in as he rode away into the darkness. He had a point. The necklace was the perfect thing to build a display around. When you thought about it, it was obvious. Franklin Oswald borrowed the Midnight Star all those years ago because he knew people would come to the Beryl just to get a glimpse. I felt in my bag. Yes, Franklin Oswald's journal was still there. I'd been too caught up in Della's case to read it through.

I unlocked the door and pushed my bike inside, trying to keep it close to the wall so the melting ice wouldn't go all over the floor. It didn't matter if I believed that the necklace was gone. I didn't have any proof. Oswald might have been obsessed with finding the Star, but just because he was crazy didn't automatically make him wrong.

CHAPTER

20

'd had the house to myself for all of fifteen minutes when there was a sharp knock on the door. An unfriendly three-beat rap that made me frown. I opened the door to find Della scowling on the threshold.

'Mom's upset,' she said, stepping into the room. I looked into the street behind her.

'She's not here,' Della said, enunciating so clearly I could hear the 'stupid' she left off the end of the sentence. 'I took a cab. Mom's at the theatre finishing Vivian's ballgown.'

I winced. 'I told you she wouldn't like it if she found out I was on the case.'

Della flipped her hair, letting me know it wasn't her fault Mom found out.

'What did she say?' I asked.

'Nothing.'

My heart skipped several beats. That was bad. If Mom was annoyed with me, she might complain to Della. But she'd never say anything if she was really upset.

Della clicked her tongue against her teeth. 'Don't worry so much. She'll get over it.'

That was easy for Della to say. She and Mom fought all the time, the way a mother and daughter are supposed to. They got angry and then made up and it was over. Maybe it was because they lived together or because they had so much in common. They could go see a show and bond over the bad lighting design. My stomach sank, like it was trying to crawl under my liver and hide. Mom and I didn't have anything like that.

But Della hadn't come to see how I was feeling.

'So,' she said, her eyebrow raised in a perfect question mark. 'Have you figured it out? Do you know who's behind the trouble?'

I closed my eyes and counted up in prime numbers trying to keep my frustration from showing. I only got to 23.

'No.' I said the word with a sigh. Della's face tightened and I added quickly, 'Not yet.'

'Why not? You've been investigating for days.'

'Yeah, two of them,' I snapped. 'It's not like the bad guy is going around wearing an "it was me" shirt.'

Della made a disgusted sound. I started to tell her to give it a rest, and then I realized what she'd said. Della had said *who*.

'You don't think it's a ghost any more?'

Della crossed her arms, hugging herself. 'Ghosts don't start rumours. That's something only a living person would do.'

It was odd. I would have expected her to look relieved. A person is a lot less scary than a ghost. Then I realized the real problem. If it was a person, it was someone at the Beryl. Someone Della knew and trusted had betrayed her.

I let out a deep breath. 'I'm sorry.'

Della blinked. 'Excuse me?'

'I'm sorry,' I said again. 'I know you didn't want it to be one of them.'

I walked around the counter into the kitchen and got two mugs out and started to warm up some milk. Della perched delicately on one of the stools across from me. She cupped her chin in her hands and rested her elbows on the Formica. She stared at me.

'What?' I asked. The spoon I was using to mix the cocoa clinked sharply against the mug.

'Apologizing is so not you. I like it,' Della practically purred. 'Do it again?'

I gave Della the sternest look I could muster and she shrugged it off like it was made of air. 'So what's up?'

I told Della about the case. I told her about almost catching the culprit yesterday in the dark, and about Benji and how he'd been making calls to Kingdom Cinemas' head office.

'And then I came back and got told off for not making the lobby display dramatic enough.'

'Linda has a point,' Della said. She held up her hands quickly. 'She could have been more tactful, but she didn't know you were there.'

I took a sip of cocoa and grumbled. 'Kevin thinks I should make it all about the Midnight Star.' I glanced at Della over the rim of my cup.

She nodded thoughtfully. 'It's not a bad idea.'

'Maybe not, but I'm not sure how to do it. Sensation and spectacle aren't exactly my strong suits.'

'Are you asking for help?'

'Maybe.'

Della looked at me, pretending to think about it.

'Make me another cup of cocoa and you've got yourself a deal.'

I spent the next hour in Dad's office, typing furiously as Della dictated splashy copy to go with each display item I'd found. She had Dad's talent for spinning a story, if not his dedication to fact-checking. On the table next to the computer, Oswald's journal and the pile of newspaper clippings he'd collected in his lifelong search for the jewel lay untouched. Every time I suggested we use one, Della waved her hand in disgust.

'You keep making it sound like the Midnight Star is still hidden in the Beryl,' I complained.

'That's the point. No one's going to get excited about a stolen necklace unless there's a chance it can be found.'

'But the chances—'

Della cut me off. 'It's the theatre, Alice. People come to see a show to escape reality. They don't want facts and figures and most-likely scenarios. They want excitement and adventure. Our job as entertainers is to give them what they want. So stop trying to make this a history report and just go with it.' She put her hands on her hips and stared down at me. Daring me to contradict her. I didn't.

'What are my two favourite girls up to in here?' Dad stood in the doorway.

'Della's helping me be sensational,' I said, my voice dry as the Sahara desert. 'How was your day? Did you manage to get an interview with that Interpol agent?'

'No,' Dad said. 'He's been dodging me all day. I think he's working undercover at one of the venues, but I can't figure out where. This guy is good.'

Dad shook his head ruefully. 'I was going to order pizza. Della, can you stay for dinner?'

Della could. Between her and Dad and a half-pepperoni half-mushroom-and-olive pizza, we finished the copy for the lobby display together.

When we finished, Dad offered to give Della a ride back to the hotel.

'Only if you go warm up the car first,' my sister said.

'As you wish,' Dad said with a courtly bow and headed out into the cold.

I heard the Plymouth splutter to life.

'You are such a diva.'

Della rolled her eyes and gave me a hug. 'Don't worry about Mom, OK?' she said. 'She'll understand.'

There was a sudden lump in my throat. That was easy for Della to say. She hadn't called Mom's dresses stupid. Or said she didn't care if the Beryl was turned into a Cineplex. I winced. I'd only said it because I'd been so mad. And it wasn't even true, not really. I didn't care about the Beryl for me, but Mom and Della did and so I cared about it for them. That was why I was investigating in the first place, to stop whoever was trying to ruin the show.

The horn beeped and Della gave me one last squeeze.

'Thanks,' I managed. The lump made my voice husky.

I locked the door behind my sister and leant my forehead against the cool wood. Maybe if I apologized to Mom in the morning, I'd stop feeling like such a toad. I took a deep breath and went back to Dad's office to gather up Oswald's papers and print out what we'd written. I had to admit, the new labels were much more exciting, even if the lack of facts set my teeth on edge.

'*But you can't prove it, can you?*

Kevin's words rattled in my brain like an ice-cream headache.

I'd been through Oswald's papers and his journal. All his

entries and the papers he'd gathered pointed to the Midnight Star still being in the Beryl. The problem was, Oswald started out already believing that the necklace was still there. It's bad logic to start with an idea and set out to prove it. It makes you miss things.

I stopped.

A slow spring of something cold crept up my spine.

Starting with an assumption is no way to solve a mystery. It's also exactly what I'd been doing ever since Della asked me to look into the problems at the Beryl.

I had assumed someone was trying to sabotage the show.

But those weren't the facts. The facts were that things were going wrong. Props misplaced, dressing rooms searched, the set mysteriously dismantled. I had assumed this meant someone was trying to spook the cast and ruin the show.

Vivian thought it was the unhappy ghost of Kittie Grace, I thought it was sabotage, but there was another explanation as well. It had been staring me in the face since I started going through the gas house, but I'd been too focused on my own assumptions to see it.

What if it wasn't someone trying to ruin the show? What if it was someone trying to find the Midnight Star?

It was the first thing Kevin had asked. Was the Star still there? The chances of that being true were x approaching 0, but it was like Della said, the truth didn't matter. An image of the Midnight Star shimmered in my memory. If the right person thought there was even a one per cent chance they could find the necklace, they'd go looking.

I stood in the middle of Dad's office with my mouth hanging open. That explained why all the problems involved things from the original production. Those were the most likely places for the necklace to be hidden. I couldn't believe I'd missed something so important. I took a breath, trying to slow my runaway train of thought. I didn't want to make the same mistake again, making assumptions and moulding the facts to fit them.

When Dad got back, he found me sitting cross-legged on the carpet in front of the couch surrounded by all Oswald's papers. I had my notebook open and was writing down all the facts I could find about the original disappearance of the Midnight Star. There weren't a lot. Some of what Oswald had gathered were eye-witness statements, but most were second- and even third-hand reports.

'Did you think of something?' Dad asked, hanging up his coat.

'Maybe,' I said slowly, still staring at Franklin Oswald's journal.

Most of the entries weren't very helpful. Random lists of suspects and places he'd searched, but nothing to explain why. Mr Oswald had horrible cramped handwriting and as the pages went on, it became sharper and more erratic, as if his frustration was actually leaking out of his pen.

The page I was looking at was about halfway through the book, where the journal naturally fell open. As if Mr Oswald had spent a lot of time rereading that particular entry.

The necklace went missing first!

The words were underlined three times and ink speckled the paper.

'What's that mean?' Dad asked, peering over my shoulder. He'd put coffee on and the smell warmed the air.

'I'm not sure.' I glanced around the newspaper clippings, all variations on the same theme – FIRE AT THE BERYL: MIDNIGHT STAR GOES MISSING. 'Everyone says there was a fire and the necklace went missing in the confusion. But if the necklace went missing first and then the fire started . . .' I trailed off.

Did that make a difference? I could feel a headache starting to form at the base of my neck. I leant back against the couch and stared up at the ceiling, trying to think. Then I shoved the papers away in frustration.

'It doesn't matter. All these papers are just sensationalism anyway. The fire was over a hundred years ago.'

'You know' – Dad tapped a finger to his chin – 'if you want facts, I could get you the old police file from the fire and the theft.'

'Can you do that?'

'I can do anything.' Dad wiggled his eyebrows at me. The coffee beeped and Dad moved to the kitchen, taking down two mugs and filling them. 'Cases that old are in the police archive. They're public record. Anyone can make a request. I'll pick you up a copy while I'm at the station.'

I took the mug he handed me gratefully.

'Thanks, Dad.'

I wasn't sure if it would do any good, but at least with a police record I'd be dealing with facts. I sipped the coffee and sighed blissfully. It would be like having my feet back on solid ground.

CHAPTER

21

I got to the Beryl early and smiled. For the first time in weeks, the bricks were clean. I pulled out my phone. Benji was clearly afraid of his mom finding out about what he'd been up to, so now I could finally get some answers. I texted him to meet me outside the Beryl at noon and not to be late.

Kevin pedalled up just as I hit 'send'.

'You look happy. What's up?'

I told him and watched the smile bloom across his face.

'Oh man, you should have told me. Do you think they sell paint at the Seven–Eleven?' Visions of revenge danced in Kevin's eyes and I held up my hand.

'We're not going to prank the kid. I need to ask him some questions.'

'Oh, come on, please?' Kevin made a face like a

wounded puppy.

'No,' I said firmly and walked across the street, up the steps of the Beryl and knocked on the door.

Kevin jogged behind me. 'Good to see you're feeling better.'

Della opened the door before I had a chance to reply. I blinked.

'Where's Jarvis?' I asked, confused.

Della's face was a few shades paler than usual, her large eyes deep with worry.

'He went with Linda to talk to the police.'

'What happened?'

'Someone broke in last night. They ripped up Mom's dress. Come on.'

Without waiting for a reply, Della grabbed my arm and pulled me into the lobby. She locked the door after Kevin and dragged us through the lobby to the costume work-shop. Mom was standing outside the open door. Two angry splotches of pink coloured her face.

I had a sudden horrible sensation, like climbing to the top of the stairs and taking one step too many. I remem-bered what I'd said before I ran out of the theatre. What if Mom thought I'd ripped up the dress? I swallowed hard, or tried to, my mouth was suddenly dry.

'Mom, Alice is here,' Della said.

I couldn't bring myself to look Mom in the eyes, so I looked past her into the costume workshop. It was worse than I'd thought. The floor was littered with long strips of blue silk and scraps of antique lace. Someone had knocked over Mom's sewing box and scissors, fabric pencils and small straight pins flashed dangerously. What was left of the ballgown still hung on the dressmaker's dummy. The bodice was mostly intact, but the skirt was in tatters.

Mom looked up and I braced myself.

'Oh, Alice, isn't it horrible?' She gestured at the mess inside the costume workshop. 'Who on earth would destroy such a beautiful dress?'

She looked at me without a trace of suspicion and the relief hit me like a bus. I let out a breath I didn't even know I was holding. I crossed the space between us in three swift steps and gave my mom a fierce hug.

'Alice?'

'I thought you'd think it was me,' I said, my face muffled in her shirt.

Mom looked down at me, shocked. 'Alice, honey, how could you think that?'

I shrugged. 'After what I said . . .'

Mom shook her head and her sea-glass earrings flashed turquoise at me. 'Last night we had a fight. I know you were upset, but I also know you wouldn't do something like this. My goodness, Alice, for such a logical child you have an awfully big imagination.'

I felt my face go hot and I swallowed hard.

Mom pulled me back against her and gave me another

tight squeeze. Behind me I was acutely aware of Kevin being way too quiet. I wondered how much teasing he'd milk this for later, and decided I didn't care.

'Come on,' Mom said after a moment. 'Let's get this place cleaned up.' She led the way into the room, stooping every few steps to pick up scraps of blue silk and lace, sighing and tutting over the waste of such good material. I kept quiet until I got the lump in my throat under control. Then I went to help Kevin tidy up the sewing box.

'It's so strange,' Mom said, picking up a long strip of fabric. 'They cut out all the seams.

'Why's that strange?' I asked.

Della picked up the last piece of lace and laid it on the sewing table, then she flopped down on the couch, clearly exhausted. 'If someone wanted to ruin the dress all they needed to do would be to cut it up with scissors. Cutting out the seams takes time.'

I nodded slowly, remembering the jacket Mom had been working on for Matthew Strange. The one with the hidden pockets stitched into the lining. Cutting out the seams didn't make sense if someone was just trying to ruin the dress. It only made sense if someone was looking for something hidden inside it.

'Was the dress ruined when you got here this morning?'

Mom clicked her teeth and nodded. 'It's so annoying. After all that trouble to do a fitting with Vivian. And I stayed late last night to finish it too. Now I'll have to start over. It will take me all day to reconstruct.' She got out a large sheet of paper from a pile under the sewing table and cleared space for it on top.

'How late did you stay?' I asked, trying to keep my voice casual.

'Around eleven.' As she answered the question, Mom looked up from her paper and narrowed her eyes at me. 'Alice, are you *investigating*?' She pivoted ninety degrees on the spike of her stiletto heel to face me. 'I told you I want you to leave this alone.'

I swallowed hard.

'It isn't her fault, Mom,' Della said. 'I asked her to do it.'

'Della!' Mom sounded shocked but Della stood her ground.

'This is important. Someone's trying to ruin the show. You know there's something going on. Alice is good at figuring things out.'

'Della, this isn't a game. This is serious. Linda has gone to see the police. They'll take care of it.'

I gritted my teeth. I didn't think the police would be showing up with sirens blazing to investigate the case of the damaged dress. Della started to protest, but I shook my head. Mom wasn't going to change her mind. Besides, she'd already told me what I needed to know. The dress had been fine when she'd left at eleven and it had been in tatters when she arrived at eight this morning. That left a nine-hour window when the culprit could have committed the crime.

The door to the costume workshop slapped open and I spun around, expecting to see riot police kicking in the door.

Vivian Rollins stood in the doorway, her face a mask of horror. She looked at the dress, her mouth open in a silent scream, and brought her hand up to her mouth. She looked like a silent-film star who'd just seen something unspeakable crawling out of a crypt.

'It's her. I knew it, it's Kittie Grace. She *is* mad.' Vivian looked around the room wildly, as if the ghost of Kittie Grace was going to swoop out of the walls and carry her away. 'I never should have agreed to reprise her role.' She took three halting steps backwards, never once taking her eyes off the dress and then she turned and fled. Her footsteps echoed down the hall.

Mom sighed. 'I wanted to get this fixed before she saw it. Della, can you go try to calm her down? I'll call Linda, but it might take her some time.'

Della nodded grimly. She started to leave and then came back and grabbed Kevin by the arm. 'Come on, Prince Charming,' she said. 'Let's use those dimples for good for a change.'

Kevin gave me a pleading look as Della dragged him out the door.

Mom watched them go. Then she sat down at the sewing table, cracked her knuckles and got to work sketching.

I watched for a minute over her shoulder. I'd seen the costumes Mom had designed before, but I'd never seen her actually designing. At first it was just what I expected. Mom drew a picture of a dress, making notes about colours and fabric types and odd terms like *gusset* and *godet*. Then she did something strange. She started drawing shapes. Not dress shapes, but geometry shapes, circles and triangles, rectangles and trapezoids. Every now and again she'd refer to a list of measurements in a small notebook and then she'd add numbers to the edge of each shape.

'What are you doing?' I asked.

Mom looked at me like I'd asked her how to do long division.

'I'm making a pattern.'

I leant in to get a better view.

'Look.' Mom unrolled a bolt of blue silk. She must have bought it to match the ballgown. 'Fabric is two-dimensional, but the person wearing it is three. You need to cut the fabric and sew it together to give it shape.'

'It's geometry,' I said quietly.

Mom blinked, tilting her head to one side. 'I guess so,' she agreed.

I'd always thought I was the only one in the family who liked maths. Della couldn't stand the subject and told me so as often as she could fit it into the conversation. Dad didn't think I was weird for liking it, but he wasn't that interested himself. I'd always assumed Mom was the same.

I did a double take as she took a compass out of her pencil case and used it to draw a perfect arc along the edge of one of the rectangles. Maybe I'd been wrong. I pulled my stool a little closer and watched. If I thought very hard, I could almost imagine all those trapezoids and triangles lifting off the page and joining together, building the shape of the dress that had been destroyed.

'That's pretty neat,' I paused. 'I'm sorry I said your dresses were stupid.'

Mom finished drawing a few more lines. 'That's OK, honey. I shouldn't have insisted you wear something you don't like. It's just that I've made so many for Della. I wanted to be able to design a dress for you too. But I understand if you don't want that.'

My chest felt tight. I tried to keep my mouth shut, but it was no use. I couldn't stop myself.

'I'd like you to design me something for opening night.'

Mom sat up straight. 'Really, you mean it?' She threw her arms around me and squeezed me so tight I couldn't speak. 'Just you wait, honey. I'm going to make you something stunning. You won't regret it!'

I wasn't so sure. But Mom looked so happy. How bad could one night in a dress really be?

CHAPTER

22

I spent the next hour in the costume workshop. Mom showed me how to draft a pattern and I helped her start mending the ballgown. Linda stuck her head in just after ten.

'Any luck with the police?' Mom asked without looking up from her whirring sewing machine.

Linda carried a heavy cardboard box with two staplers balanced on top. She shook her head ruefully. 'They've taken my statement.'

Like I'd thought, the police weren't interested. To them it was just some worthless dress, but not to me. I'd seen how much it meant to my mom and I was going to find the person responsible.

'Vivian saw the mess,' Mom said.

Linda flinched, almost sending the staplers to the floor.

'I sent Della to calm her down. But you might want to go check on her.'

'Right,' Linda said, and turned to leave.

'I'll go with you,' I said. Kevin hadn't come back yet and I was worried he might need to be rescued.

I followed Linda down the hall towards the dressing rooms. Silence hung between us, heavy and uncomfortable. Linda cleared her throat.

'I wanted to apologize for yesterday. I shouldn't have taken my frustration out on you. You've been such a help, Alice, we really do appreciate it. I hope you know that.'

Warmth spread out from the middle of my chest. I nodded.

'And don't worry about the display. I'm sure if we all work together—'

'It's OK,' I cut in. 'Della helped me write some new labels, all about the mystery of the Midnight Star. Trust me, it's sensational.'

Linda nodded approvingly. 'I like the angle. OK. Let me know when it's done and I'll have a look.'

We found Vivian in her dressing room. She sat at her dressing table rocking slightly in her chair. Della sat at her feet speaking in a low soothing voice. Kevin was nowhere to be seen.

'Della, Vivian,' Linda said. 'Frank is waiting to start rehearsal.'

Vivian closed her eyes. For a moment I thought she was

going to say no, but then she took a deep shuddering breath and opened her eyes. She even managed a weak smile.

'The show must go on?'

Linda nodded and Della took Vivian's hand and the two actresses left together. Della eyeballed me over her shoulder. Her thoughts were so clear I wondered if she'd been taking a mime class: *You need to put a stop to this. Now!*

She was right.

Vivian was highly strung to begin with, so another scare might make her snap. And just telling her there are no such things as ghosts wasn't going to cut it. I needed to find the human behind the 'haunting' and expose them.

Linda put the box she'd been carrying down with a heavy thump. 'It's Cragthorne, it has to be. He can't file any more injunctions so he's taking direct action.' She turned to me. 'What about that confession you were talking about last night? Do you have it? If I can show that to the police maybe they'll do something.'

Kevin came around the corner in the middle of Linda's speech, carrying a bag from 7– Eleven.

'I'll have it soon,' I said quickly. 'After lunch.'

Linda checked the time and scowled. 'Fine. Until then, you can fold programmes. I need to call our lawyer. I want him ready to go as soon as I have proof of what Mr Cragthorne is up to.'

She handed me the box and gave Kevin the staplers,

then she strode out of the office dialling her phone.

I swallowed hard. Hoping I was right about Benji.

'Where did you go?' I asked as Kevin came into the room. 'And what's that smell?'

'Ghost repellent.' He pulled a garlic chilli hot dog out of the bag and laid it on Vivian's make-up table. The smell made my eyes water. 'They didn't have any of the fresh stuff.'

'Garlic is for vampires,' I said.

Kevin shrugged. 'Pot-ay-to pot-ah-to. It'll make her feel better.'

I wasn't so sure. 'Come on, help me with these programmes.'

After five minutes the smell of garlic was too much. We moved to the lobby and set up on the floor, putting programme sheets in a pile, stapling them in the middle and folding them in half.

I tried to keep focused on the pages in front of me, but I couldn't help worrying. If the things going wrong at the Beryl were just someone searching for the Midnight Star, then Cragthorne might not have anything to do with it. Maybe he hadn't paid Benji to graffiti the building either.

My phone rang and I jumped. I was still getting used to having it back.

'Hi, sweetie,' Dad said. 'I'm just leaving the police

station. Want me to swing by with the files?'

'You got them?'

'Of course I got them. I've got the posters too. They look pretty snazzy if I do say so myself.'

I thought for a minute. Normally I would have told Dad to bring the files home instead of coming to the theatre. It wasn't like my mom and dad fought or anything, but it was just weird to see them together. Like brushing your teeth after drinking orange juice. I never knew what to say or where to stand. But I really wanted those files, and I needed the signs for the lobby display.

'I'll meet you out front,' I said.

Dad told me he'd be at the Beryl in five minutes. I got Kevin to stand by the Stage Door for me and I waited outside until I saw the Plymouth peel around the corner. It was a boxy, brick-coloured car with wood panelling on the doors. Dad hit the brakes hard and screeched to a stop right in front of the stairs.

I jogged down the alley and leant in Dad's car window.

'Here.' Dad handed me a stack of photocopied papers from the passenger's seat followed by a large parcel wrapped in brown packing paper. It barely fitted through the window. He was smiling so hard I could see his back teeth.

'I guess your meeting with the detective went well?'

Dad's eyes glistened. 'On the record, it was OK. But off the record, he confirmed that Interpol is in town and they suspect the thief is planning something big. The sapphires must have been a warm-up. I'm betting it's tonight at the Snow Ball at City Hall. Can you have dinner with your mom tonight?'

I nodded.

'OK. Love you.'

I jumped back just in time to avoid the spray of slush as Dad hit the gas, skidding slightly as he sped up the road.

Inside, I dropped the parcel on the lobby floor and flipped through the photocopied pages of the police reports. They were handwritten, the letters small and extremely neat.

'What's that?' Kevin asked, looking over my shoulder.

'It's the original police and fire reports from the night the Midnight Star went missing.'

'I thought you were supposed to make the display *less* like a history report.'

'I know. This isn't for the display. *That* is.' I nudged the package with my toe and Kevin knelt down to untie the twine holding it together.

Inside were a pile of newspapers, not real newspapers but mock-ups of the copy Della and Dad had helped me write, printed on thick posterboard. Dad had even used some of the photographs I'd found in the gas house. I had to admit, it looked pretty good.

The police files weren't nearly as glamorous. But they were true. To me that made them miles more interesting than some story Della and Dad and I had made up. Even if the story version had more glitz and glamour and even a ghost.

Kevin lifted up the top board and the face of Kittie Grace peered out from under the lurid headline THE BEAUTIFUL GHOST OF THE BERYL: DOES KITTIE GRACE STILL TREAD THESE BOARDS? He covered it up again quickly. 'Maybe we should wait to put that one up until later?'

I thought of Vivian rocking back and forth in her dressing-room chair and agreed. We could hang that one on opening night, once Vivian was safely backstage.

'Well, let's get started.' I put down the police file reluctantly.

'Do you think there's a clue in there?' Kevin asked.

I shrugged. 'Probably not. I was just trying to understand what happened.'

Kevin raised a disbelieving eyebrow. 'Read it. I'll hang up the posters.'

'I'm not five. I can wait.'

'Yeah, but there might be something in there. Besides, you don't have my flair for the dramatic.'

Kevin bowed low, twirling his wrist like an eighteenth-century duke. I couldn't help laughing.

'Suit yourself. Pete's got mounting tape in the workshop.' I grabbed the file before Kevin could change his mind and tucked myself into the corner.

I skimmed through the police report first. And as I read,

my eyes grew wider. Franklin Oswald had been right. The Midnight Star had gone missing first.

The first page of the report was written by a constable who'd been in the audience on opening night. The language was old-fashioned, but I got the gist of it. The Midnight Star was put in a safe onstage at the end of Act One, but when the maid went to take it out again at the beginning of Act Two, it wasn't there. At first the constable thought this was part of the show, but when the actors started miming that the necklace was there, he realized something was wrong and called for backup. The police showed up before the interval and the actors and crew who had access to the necklace were confined to the stage.

The next report was from a more senior officer. Apparently all the cast and crew were searched, but none of them had the necklace. They were preparing to search the set when the fire broke out and the theatre was evacuated.

There were lists of suspects. The lead actor was a known gambler, one of the stagehands had connections to the Mob, but it didn't look like they got any further than that.

The fire destroyed any real evidence, and since Franklin Oswald paid the original owner for losing the necklace, the police didn't officially have a crime to investigate.

The fire report was less of a surprise. The investigator concluded that the fire had started when a limelight was knocked over by a faulty sandbag. The fire spread very quickly due to the chemicals in the light and the only reason there weren't more deaths was due to the fact that the show had been stopped and most of the theatregoers had already left.

Kittie Grace had been found near the limelight that started the blaze. The coroner concluded that she'd been too close to the fire's point of origin to escape, although he couldn't say if she'd been beside the light when it fell or if she had gone back to try to put the fire out.

Or maybe she'd gone back to get the Midnight Star out of its hiding spot.

I reread the entire file again, more carefully this time, but nothing new jumped out. I closed my eyes and tried to sort out the facts. If the necklace had gone missing first, that meant someone had planned to steal it, not that someone grabbed it in the confusion of the fire. The constable must have really put a kink in their plans.

I stopped, flipping back through the pages.

The constable prevented everyone from going back to their dressing rooms. Everyone was searched while they were still onstage. And the diamond was never found. I looked at the floor plan of the set in the back of the file. The safe was in the middle of the upper level on the stage. So whoever stole the Star had to have been one of the people the police searched. I did a quick calculation. But no matter how I arranged the facts, the answer came out the same. The reason the Midnight Star wasn't found was because the thief must have hidden it. And the only place they could have hidden it was somewhere on the Beryl's stage.

CHAPTER

23

I stared blankly at the police file. It wasn't possible, it couldn't be. But facts don't lie.

Kevin had finished hanging the fake newspapers around the lobby, moving the replica of the Midnight Star to the centre of the room. It sparkled in the sunlight like it was winking at me. He'd moved the vitrified sandbag to the far corner of the lobby under the headline: THE BERYL ABLAZE. I sighed. I guess I was the only one who thought that the chemical reaction from the broken limelight was interesting.

Kevin held the door to the main theatre open and Pete shuffled through, a roll of electrical cable over his shoulder and a gigantic toolbox in one hand. He wore all black, as usual, and his T-shirt read: *Stagehand is Just Another Word for Ninja.* Pete deposited the wire and toolbox on the ground and went back into the theatre.

'What's that?' I asked Kevin, nodding to the pile Pete had left in the middle of the floor.

'Pete said he'd set up some lights. Downlighting or something?'

I nodded absently. 'Kevin, how much do you think that necklace would be worth if someone found it today?'

'I don't know, a couple of million at least.' Kevin eyed me suspiciously. 'Why?'

'Just curious,' I said quickly. I didn't want Kevin to start tearing the place apart searching for the Midnight Star just yet. There was already one person doing that, and they were causing enough trouble all by themselves. I looked at my phone. It was almost noon. 'Come on,' I said. 'It's time for Benji to face the music.'

Kevin and I waited outside the Beryl, sitting on the cold dry steps of the building. Kevin stomped his feet, but I barely felt the cold, I was too busy going over the case in my head. All the 'disturbances' at the Beryl could be explained by someone searching for something: the props that were misplaced and the set pieces that were tampered with, Della's searched dressing room, even Mom's ballgown being ripped up.

And if someone was searching for the Midnight Star, that explained why all the trouble was focused on things from the original production. Those were the only places where the thief could have hidden the Star back in 1927.

I sucked in a breath so sharply the cold made my teeth ache.

There was something else all those props and set pieces and costumes had in common. Kittie Grace. The props on my list were all ones she'd used, and so were the set pieces, and the costumes. They were all places where Kittie Grace could have hidden the Midnight Star.

No wonder Vivian thought the actress's ghost was after her.

Kevin nudged me and I looked up, following the line of his finger down the road.

A short figure in a familiar hooded parka shuffled up the pavement towards the theatre. He kept darting looks over his shoulder, like he was worried someone was following him. Kevin bounced excitedly in his seat.

'Be cool. Even if he's annoying, we need him to talk. OK? I need you to back me up.'

Kevin sighed, but he stopped bouncing. 'All right, all right, but only because you asked nicely.'

'Hello, Benji,' I said, when he finally got to where we were waiting. I hoped using his nickname would put him in a cooperative mood. 'My name is Alice. This is Kevin. It's nice to meet you.'

Kevin crossed his arms and tried to look intimidating. The problem was, he had dimples even when he scowled. Benji didn't look impressed.

'What do you want?' Benji asked. He sounded even younger than he looked.

'I want to know why you've been spray-painting the Beryl.'

Benji shrugged. 'I'm an artist and Philly is my canvas.'

'I don't think illegally defacing property is considered art.'

'A square like you wouldn't understand. I'm gonna be the next Banksy. You just can't handle my message.'

The muscles in my jaw tightened and I counted up in primes. No matter how much I wanted to push him into a slush pile, I needed to keep my cool. Beside me, Kevin's shoulders shook with suppressed laughter. The traitor.

'I don't think that's the whole story. I mean, why the Beryl? It's an awful long bike ride from your house.'

'I was following my muse.'

Benji looked like butter wouldn't melt in his mouth, so I hit him with my best shot.

'I know you're working for Rex Cragthorne. You've been calling him every morning.'

Benji looked up, shocked. His eyes were startlingly grey. 'You went through my phone?! You can't do that! It's illegal!'

'You *stole* my phone,' I shouted, stepping forward and poking the kid in the chest with my finger.

Kevin put his hand on my shoulder. 'Alice, look, Benji's not going to talk. He's got principles. He's an artist.'

Benji nodded. 'What he said. He gets it.'

I glared at Kevin, I couldn't believe he was siding with

that punk.

'Well, if he doesn't want to talk, maybe I'll just ask his mom what she knows.' I lifted my phone.

'No!' Benji shouted before he could stop himself.

Kevin pushed my hand down. 'There's no need for that.' He jogged down the steps and put his arm around Benji's shoulder. 'You're an artist, Benji. A rebel. I respect that. What I don't understand is how you could take orders from The Man.'

'What are you talking about?'

'Rex Cragthorne is Big Business. He's Corporate America. He's trying to ruin the Beryl. Face it, Benji, you sold out.'

Benji put a finger to his lips and tapped it three times. 'I hadn't thought about it like that.'

'And now here you are, protecting his secret. You're his puppet.' Kevin winked at me. I rolled my eyes. I couldn't believe this was working.

'Hey, I'm nobody's puppet. I'll tell you what I know,' Benji said defiantly, then added, 'Don't tell my mom, OK?'

I nodded and put away my phone.

'OK, so I was, uh, painting a mural outside the Kingdom Cinema on Gerrard when this huge security guard grabbed me. I thought for sure they would call my mom and then I'd be grounded until I turned forty.

'Anyway, after ages, Cragthorne showed up. He said he'd forget all about me spray-painting his movie theatre if I found a different place to paint. And then he mentioned the Beryl. So I thought, why not? I was gonna paint some-thing anyway, might as well be somewhere that would keep me out of trouble.'

'And you liked it so much you kept coming back?'

'No. After the first time, Cragthorne called me. I had to give him my number – that was part of the deal. Anyway, he said it was cleaned off and he'd give me free movie tickets if I sprayed it again. But this time he told me what to say.'

'Let me get this straight. You've been tagging the Beryl for free movie passes?'

Benji shook his head like he was ashamed of himself. For taking the bribe, not for defacing public property. Like he said, he had principles.

'Well, if we're done, I've got places to be.'

'Not so fast,' I said. Just because I had a new theory about what was going on inside the Beryl didn't mean I was going to stop investigating every possibility. 'Did Cragthorne ever ask you to do anything inside the Beryl?'

'No way. I am strictly a brick man, I don't do interiors.'

'What about your hideout?' Kevin asked.

'Oh well, yeah, but that's it. I've never been inside the Beryl.'

I nodded. 'Do you know if Cragthorne asked anyone else to cause trouble inside?'

'I don't know. Why would he tell me?' Benji looked at me like I was too stupid to have lived to be twelve.

I gritted my teeth and reminded myself to breathe.

'Think. Maybe you overheard something?'

'Nope,' Benji said. 'Can I go now?'

'Not yet,' Kevin said. 'We need you to come with us and talk to the woman in charge of the Beryl.'

Benji took a step back, slipping and catching himself before he fell. 'You can't do that, you said you weren't gonna get me in trouble.'

Kevin kept his arm firmly around Benji's shoulder and ushered him towards the Stage Door.

'Don't worry, kid. As long as you don't spray-paint the building again, Linda will forgive you. She might even commission a painting. She's a big supporter of the arts.'

We escorted Benji directly to Linda's office. I didn't trust letting him out of my sight. Linda took one look at Benji and whisked him out of the theatre for lunch. I guess she figured she'd get more information out of him if chocolate cake was on the menu. Then Kevin and I headed back to the lobby.

We'd only been gone half an hour, but with a few lighting rigs and a lot of spotlight bulbs, Pete had transformed it from a plain white box full of glass cabinets to a sleek stylish room full of treasure. Clear white light shone down on to each display. If I thought a glass case made the original script look good, a glass case and a spotlight made it look ready for the red carpet.

Besides the spotlight, Pete had also set up some general

lighting, creating a subtle path through the display, leading from one case to the next in a large loop and finishing
at the replica of the Midnight Star.

'Nice job, Pete,' Kevin said.

Pete beamed. 'My pleasure. This is a great display.
Linda's going to love it.' His eyes swept over the room,
drinking in all the gaudy details and came to rest on the
Midnight Star replica. Pete sighed. 'It's too bad it isn't the
real one.'

Something stirred in the back of my mind. Pete knew all
about the history of the Beryl.

'Do you think the Star's still here?' I asked as casually as
I could.

Pete ducked his head and rubbed the back of his neck
with one hand; the other rested on his hip. He looked
more embarrassed than suspicious. 'It might be,' he said. 'I
like to think it is. But if Franklin Oswald didn't find it, I don't
think anyone ever will. That man searched this building
from top to bottom. He tore down the whole set looking
for hiding places.' Pete blushed a shade of red so deep it
was almost purple. 'I checked too, when I put the set back
together.'

Something clicked in the back of my mind.

'You said the safe was part of the original set. Did you
notice anything odd about it after it fell? Maybe like a
secret compartment?'

I ignored Kevin's raised eyebrow and waited for Pete.

'I thought that might be the hiding spot too! But it was just a box. Why? Do *you* think the necklace is still here?'

'No,' I said. I hated to disappoint him. 'I was just curious.'

Pete waited for a moment to see if I was going to change my mind and tell him the necklace was still there and I knew where it was hiding. I didn't. If Pete had checked the whole set, that disproved my theory that the diamond was hidden there. Unless he'd missed something.

A chill passed over me as I watched Pete pack up his tools and leave the lobby. I didn't want to believe that Pete could be the one behind the problems at the Beryl, but I couldn't rule him out. I remembered the cold strong hands pushing me towards the edge of the stage in the dark and shuddered.

But no, I shook my head. It couldn't be Pete. He could have the set to himself any time he wanted. He didn't need to sneak into the Beryl at night and search it again.

I growled.

If Kittie Grace had stolen the Midnight Star and hidden it onstage, she'd done a good enough job to fool the police and everyone who'd ever searched for it since. I couldn't just assume Pete would have found it if it was there.

I had to search for it myself.

CHAPTER

24

I waited until Frank and the cast stopped for lunch, before slipping into the empty auditorium, Kevin close on my heels. My stomach growled loudly.

'What are you doing?' Kevin asked as I jogged down the aisle. I shivered slightly as I skirted the pit and vaulted up on to the stage. It looked deeper and more dangerous than ever.

'Let me know if anyone's coming,' I said to Kevin.

I closed my eyes, trying to remember what I'd heard the night I'd surprised the intruder.

'What are you—'

I held up my hand and cut Kevin off.

It had been dark, and I'd heard a sound from the stage. Like someone pulling nails out of a plank of wood. I'd thought the intruder was messing with the set, but it had been fine when the lights came on. I thought that was because I'd scared them off, but maybe not.

There had been footsteps, muffled at first like they'd been over carpet, and then louder. I moved backwards until the sounds matched, hoping that Kevin would shout if I was about to step off the edge of the stage. There. The floor didn't change under my feet, but the sound did. I opened my eyes.

I was standing upstage centre, the false wall between the sitting room and the hallway to my left. I tapped my foot on the floor; it sounded hollow.

I crouched down and ran my fingers over the floorboards. It was an old stage, the floor made of strips of painted wood instead of one large flat piece of plywood. My fingers found it before my eyes, a crack that was a little larger than the others, and when my fingers followed it the crack traced a perfect square. On one side faint scratch marks showed where someone had tried to prise it open.

Pete kept a spare toolbox in the wings for set emergencies. I rifled through it and found a crowbar and then ran back to centre stage.

'What are you doing?' Kevin asked from behind me and I jumped clear off the ground.

'You're supposed to be keeping a lookout,' I said, trying to shove my stomach back down where it belonged.

'No one's coming.'

I knelt down and tucked the thin end of the crowbar into the crack, using it as a lever. There was a horrible screeching sound, just like the one I'd heard two nights ago.

A large dark square yawned open beneath us.

I leant into the darkness. I could see a small square of dark ground about a metre and a half below me, but nothing else.

Kevin pulled me back. 'Are you kidding me?' he asked. 'If we were in a movie, this is the part where the whole audience would be screaming *don't go down there!*'

'This isn't a movie,' I said, but when I looked down into the darkness my stomach quivered. If there were such things as ghosts, this is exactly where they'd hide. I swallowed hard, I wasn't about to tell Kevin I was scared of something I didn't even believe in. I swung my legs into the hole and half slid, half jumped into the darkness below.

I landed with a small thump. The light from above barely touched the gloom, so I held up my phone for illumination. The space under the stage was too low to be called a room. I had to keep my head slightly ducked to avoid hitting the ceiling. The smell of soot hung in the air more strongly than anywhere else in the theatre.

Kevin landed with a thud behind me. 'What is this place?'

I shrugged, squinting through the darkness. The ceiling had several rusted hinges along the edges that made it look like once a much larger portion of the stage floor could open.

'They might have kept sets here, or used it as another entrance for actors?'

Kevin shifted to get a closer look at the hinges.

'Wait,' I said. 'Don't move.'

I swept my phone low to the ground, lighting up the floor. A thick layer of dust covered the room from wall to wall. There were small scuff marks and footprints where Kevin and I had landed, but nothing else. I couldn't see all the way to the end of the room, so I took some quick photos of the undisturbed dust.

'What are you doing?' Kevin held on to my shoulder for balance, doing his best impression of a statue.

'No footprints,' I said. I checked the pictures and then started to walk away from the trapdoor's square of light, keeping close to the wall. I counted my steps as I went. Cobwebs brushed against my face and I tried not to imagine gigantic spiders hiding in the dark.

'So?' Kevin stayed put, standing like a singer in a spotlight.

'So no one's been down here but us. The other night when I heard someone sneaking around onstage, I must have scared them off before they had a chance to search it.'

It was twenty-five steps to the end of the room, so I estimated I was standing under the stage's left wing. A metal ladder was bolted to the wall, leading to another hatch. I climbed the seven rungs and pushed up. The trapdoor didn't budge. When I looked more closely I could see it was bolted shut. I jiggled the bolt, but it was rusted solid.

I retraced my steps back past Kevin and went to the other side of the room. An identical ladder and an identical hatch. The rust wasn't as bad on this side of the stage and I managed to work the bolt free. I lifted the trapdoor open just enough for me to peer out. I was right, the hatch came up in the stage's right wing. I closed the door and dropped back to the floor.

'Wait, if no one's been down here,' Kevin said as I came back to the square of light where he waited, 'does that mean the diamond might still be here?'

'Maybe,' I said slowly, trying not to get my hopes up. It seemed unlikely that someone as obsessed with finding the Midnight Star as Franklin Oswald wouldn't have searched here already. But I couldn't help feeling a little excited. Besides, not searching would be sloppy detective work.

Kevin clapped his hands together.

I pointed Kevin left and I took stage right, carefully walking along the perimeter of the room looking for anything that might be a hiding place for a million-dollar necklace. I didn't find anything. The walls of the room were rough, but solid with no convenient knotholes or hidden compartments. I reached the end of the wall and turned the corner, checking the area around the ladder. There was nothing there either. My shoulders were starting to ache from hunching over.

'Numbers,' Kevin called from across the room, his voice an octave higher than usual. He coughed. 'I think I found something.'

My heart kicked and I hurried towards Kevin's voice, holding up my phone to light the way. He was crouched next to a small panel in the wall, dancing from foot to foot.

'There.' He pointed excitedly. 'Do you see it? It's a door or something.'

'Well,' I said, 'aren't you going to open it?'

Kevin swallowed. Then he hooked his fingers around the edge of the panel and pulled.

The panel hadn't been opened in decades and the hinges were stiff with age. Kevin's fingernails scrabbled against the wood and I cringed at the sound. It started to ease open and then, all at once, the hinges gave way. I held up my phone, shining the electronic white light into the hole.

Something flashed in the darkness and Kevin grabbed my shoulder.

'There!' he practically yelled.

My breath caught in my throat as silver light glittered back at me. And then I looked closer.

'No,' I said, trying to keep the disappointment out of my voice.

The light flashed against a large wheel with a crank

handle. Three levers stuck out of the wall to its right. Kevin stuck his face into the hole, craning his neck and checking every corner.

'Anything?' I asked, even though I knew the answer.

Kevin shook his head. He looked like someone who'd found out his chocolate cake was made of spinach. 'Nope,' he said. 'Man, I thought we'd found it.' He grabbed the handle of the crank and pulled down hard. I didn't think it would move, but the door must have protected the inner workings from the years of dust and soot. The wheel spun easily and the sound of gears cranking filled the small space under the stage. A spring released somewhere behind the wall and the trapdoor in the stage floor swung closed with a definite snap.

I dropped my phone and the room went completely black. Pale shadows danced across my vision as my eyes tried to adjust to the dark. I dropped to my knees and searched for the phone, but all I found was greasy dust.

'Turn it the other way!' I said.

Kevin grunted and gears strained but nothing happened.

'It won't go the other way.'

I thought furiously. There had to be a way to get the door open. There was no point in having a trapdoor if you couldn't open it. My hand closed on my phone and I breathed a sigh of relief and turned it on.

'Try the levers.'

'What levers?' Kevin looked relieved that I'd found the light too.

'Those.' I pointed with my phone. 'You keep trying. I'll go see if anything happens.'

I left my phone with Kevin and made my way blindly to the trapdoor, using the number of my steps to estimate the distance. Something brushed against my face and I waved wildly at the air in front of me catching my arm on one of the low beams.

'It's just a cobweb,' I said to myself. All Della and Vivian's talk of ghosts was starting to get to me.

I heard the clunk of gears shifting as Kevin pulled the lever. And suddenly the ground beneath my feet started to rise.

'Anything?' Kevin called.

'Stop,' I yelled. 'Stop!'

The ceiling was about half a metre closer than it should have been. I felt my way to the edge of a small platform, but in the dark I didn't dare step off the edge. Instead, I squatted down and wrapped my arms around my knees. The platform kept rising.

'I can't stop it, it's like a wind-up car or something.'

More cobwebs. I hunched lower as they draped across my arms and tangled in my hair.

'Try the last lever.'

Kevin hit the last gear and turned the wheel. Above me the hinges of the trapdoor protested mightily, and then as suddenly as the door had shut, it swung back open, air rustling as it skimmed past my ear. I stood up, furiously brushing the cobwebs from my hair and face and spitting them from my mouth.

'I'll take ghosts over spiders any day,' I muttered.

I knelt down to help Kevin, but as soon as my knees touched the platform a large hand clamped down on the back of my shirt, pulling me back to my feet.

'Gotcha!'

CHAPTER

25

Whoever had their hand on the back of my shirt didn't wait for a reply. They just pulled. My feet lifted off the platform and I shot up and backwards on to the stage.

'Hey!' I yelled, kicking my legs as I spun free and shoved myself backwards, crab-walking on my hands and feet. The wooden floor of the stage felt rough under my palms. I stopped as my fingers touched the edge of the hole in the stage.

'Alice?'

Jarvis stared at me, his mouth open and his expression blank. Whoever he had expected to pull out of that hole, it certainly wasn't me. His mouth snapped shut. 'What were you doing down there?'

Jarvis tried to look around me and I leant to one side,

blocking his view. There was no reason for Kevin to get caught too.

'I was just checking if anything was down there.' It was a lame excuse and I knew it, but it was the truth.

'Did you find anything?'

I frowned. That wasn't the question I'd expected.

Frank's voice boomed through the closed lobby doors and Jarvis's head snapped up. He opened his mouth and then shut it again, and threw a worried glance at the doors.

'Get this thing closed,' he said quietly. 'And then you and I are going to have a talk.'

I turned around, thinking furiously. What was Jarvis doing sneaking around the stage during lunch? And why didn't he want anyone to know about the trapdoor. For that matter, why had he been there the other night? Jarvis was way too twitchy for someone who found a kid messing around on the stage. I also needed to figure out how to get Kevin out of there without being caught.

I peered into the hole. Kevin was already gone.

'Well, get it closed,' Jarvis said again.

I grabbed the open flap of the trapdoor, prayed that Kevin had got out through the other exit and wasn't just hiding in the dark, and started to push. The gears beneath the stage screeched in protest, and the trapdoor slammed shut under my weight.

Jarvis nodded approval and checked the theatre one

more time to make sure we were still alone, then he grabbed on to my shoulder and shoved me towards the wings.

'Right, come with me.'

I stumbled slightly as Jarvis steered me backstage and into the wings. It was dark and claustrophobic between the black curtains. Jarvis looked around one more time and then turned to me.

'Who are you working for?'

Something about Jarvis's voice had changed. It wasn't creaky or cantankerous like usual. He wasn't asking because he was angry; he sounded concerned. I frowned so hard I felt a crease form between my eyes.

'What are you talking about? I'm not working for anyone.' I stopped, as that wasn't strictly true.

Jarvis sensed the pause and leant forward, pushing the issue. 'Tell me who you're working for.'

'Della,' I said bluntly.

'What?'

'My sister thought the Beryl was haunted so she asked me to look into it. I'm working for her.'

Jarvis ran his hand over his head, all the way from the bottom of his chin to the end of his short grey ponytail. 'Of course you are,' he muttered. 'Well? Did you find anything down there?' He looked at me with clear blue eyes.

I folded my arms. 'Why should I tell you? For all I know you're the one behind it all.'

Jarvis wheezed out a laugh and shook his head. 'Why would I want to do that?'

'I don't know, maybe Rex Cragthorne is paying you. Maybe you're looking for the Midnight Star. You were here two nights ago. Maybe you were just pretending to save me.'

Jarvis and I stared at each other, hard. I didn't really think it was him, but that was the second time he'd been lurking on the stage. He was hiding something. Still, there was nothing to stop him from looking through the trap-door himself. So keeping what I saw a secret didn't make much sense. Besides, sometimes the best way to get answers is to let the other person think they're the one asking all the questions.

I broke our staring contest with a shrug.

'I didn't find anything – there was just a big empty room full of dust. And no one else had been there either,' I said. 'No footprints.'

For a second, Jarvis looked impressed. Then he narrowed his eyes. 'There are footprints now, though, aren't there?'

'I took pictures. It's not like it's an active crime scene or something.'

Jarvis froze. It was just a small jerk of his head and he covered it quickly, but I didn't miss it.

'Is it?' I asked.

Jarvis leant close to me, his cracked fingernails pressing

into my upper arm. 'You're dealing with something bigger than you know. I need you to trust me and leave it alone.'

Jarvis didn't know me very well if he thought that would keep me away.

'What do you think you're doing?' Mom's voice cut through the darkness of the theatre wings. She stood silhouetted by the stage lights. Kevin stood behind her, giving me an enormous thumbs up.

Jarvis let go of my arm and took a quick step back.

'Mr Jarvis?' My mom's voice was as cold as hypothermia and twice as dangerous.

'It's OK, Mom,' I said. 'He was just asking me about the other night. To see if I remembered anything about the intruder.'

I'm not sure Mom completely believed me. Kevin had probably run to her screaming that I was being kidnapped. I walked over to her, trying to keep the wobble out of my legs.

'I was just telling your daughter to be careful around the stage. And not to go looking for trouble.'

Mom snorted and the edges of the tension around us started to melt. 'I've been telling her that since she could crawl. Come on, Alice.'

She put her arm around my shoulder and ushered me out of the wings and off the stage. Kevin followed close behind. I could feel Jarvis watching us walk away, but he didn't make a move to follow.

'Mom,' I asked when we got out of earshot, 'how did Mr Jarvis get the job as the Beryl's caretaker?'

Mom frowned. 'I don't know,' she admitted after a moment. 'He was already here when Della and I arrived from New York. Linda must have hired him.'

I turned around as we left the theatre through the lobby doors. Jarvis stood on the stage, never taking his eyes off us.

Linda loved the new theatre display. She took one look, then started taking carefully composed pictures to update the website and began tweeting like crazy about the mystery of the Midnight Star.

'I don't get why Linda still keeps trying to sell tickets. Isn't the show already sold out?' I asked. I was sitting on the couch in the costume workshop while Mom furiously ran the newly repaired ballgown through her sewing machine. Kevin had gone home blissfully happy after spending the afternoon as Matthew Strange's personal dogsbody.

'It's only sold out on opening night. If she hypes interest now, we could sell out for the whole run. Maybe they'll even have an encore performance.'

Della came into the room and leant against the door. She looked at Mom hopefully.

'I don't think so, you've got school.'

Della sighed. 'When are you going to give it up and

home-school me?'

Mom clucked. 'When you get a role that pays for a personal tutor, you can quit regular school.' She pulled the dress off the sewing machine and shook it into shape. I'd never really thought about how impressive her designs were before now. To me they were just clothes, but now that I could see how the planes of the fabric intersected to create three-dimensional shapes I had a new appreciation for how complex they were.

'Looks good, Mom,' I said.

Mom held up the dress and ran her critical eyes from top to bottom. 'It'll have to do. I'm going to find Vivian. At least *she'll* be happy. Now she doesn't have to wear the ghost dress.'

Della watched Mom go with a little shiver, as if she was still considering if the ghost might be real. Then she turned her gaze on me. 'Well?'

I groaned silently. Della wanted an update. The problem was, I didn't have anything concrete to tell her. I wasn't any closer to figuring out the mystery of the Beryl. In fact, instead of figuring out who was sabotaging the show, all I'd done was discover the problems probably weren't about sabotage at all.

'Do you know what's going on yet?'

I shook my head.

Della sat down on the couch beside me. 'Alice, this is serious. Tomorrow is dress rehearsal.'

'I know, Della, I'm sorry. There's just too many facts, and too many people. Every time I think I get close . . .' I made a small motion like sand slipping through my fingers.

'You're supposed to be good at this, Alice. If someone wants to ruin the show, tomorrow is their last chance. Something bad is going to happen, I can feel it.' My sister glared at me, hard. 'Don't roll your eyes. All you've done is mess around with the lobby and Kevin. As soon as you proved it wasn't a ghost, you didn't care any more.'

'Just because I didn't assume it was a ghost doesn't mean I'm not trying,' I said.

Della flushed beautifully, turning exactly the right shade to let me know she was really quite angry.

'I'm sorry,' I said quickly, holding up my hands. 'Look, I'm on to something, OK? I just need time to put the pieces together.'

Della looked at her watch. 'You've got twenty-four hours.'

If I wanted to be technical, it was closer to thirty hours, but I didn't think Della was being specific. I stood up. 'Tell Mom I went home early.'

I had some thinking to do.

CHAPTER

26

I woke up with my face pressed into the crease of Franklin Oswald's journal and the taste of soot in my mouth. The surface of my bed was littered with pages from the police and fire reports and a pen was sticking into my ribs.

I sat up slowly, rubbing my side with one hand and shivered. It must have been well below freezing outside, despite the bright blue sky. I swung my feet out of bed and padded across the hall to the bathroom, turning on the shower as hot as it would go.

The warm water slowly thawed my limbs. I'd stayed up late going over the case, but I hadn't gotten very far. There were too many variables. I didn't know if I was trying to solve for x or y and my mystery equation was a complete mess.

'Morning, sweetie,' Dad said as I came down the stairs. He handed me a steaming cup of coffee and slid a bowl of oatmeal across the counter as I took a seat. 'What's up, it looks like you had a rough night.'

'It's the Beryl,' I said, taking a sip. The coffee was hot and sweet.

Dad took a bite of his oatmeal and waited.

I filled Dad in on my investigation. He almost snorted coffee out his nose when I described how Kevin had sweet-talked Benji into giving up Cragthorne.

'I knew I liked that boy for a reason.' Dad's eyes glittered as he shifted into story mode. 'So you actually have proof Cragthorne was behind the graffiti?'

I nodded.

'So why aren't you more excited? That's a huge scoop.'

'Because it doesn't explain everything else that's going on. I just keep going around in circles. I know Cragthorne was behind the graffiti, but that doesn't prove he's behind the problems inside the Beryl too. It just feels like, no matter what I do, I can't find the equation that makes all the evidence fit.'

Dad frowned. He took my empty cup and bowl and put them in the sink.

'Maybe the problem is you're trying to solve one equation, when you should be trying to solve two.'

I frowned. If I took the graffiti out of the equation, the trouble at the Beryl could all be explained by someone secretly searching the set for the Midnight Star.

Dad clapped his hands together. 'Now come on, I'm

driving down to City Hall to look into all these injunctions that Cragthorne menace has been trying to file. I'll give you a ride to the theatre.'

I grabbed my coat from beside the door. 'Why are you looking into the injunctions?'

'I can't let a bully like Cragthorne destroy the Beryl. Not when both of my daughters have been working so hard to save it. Besides, between the injunctions that were denied and the graffiti, I think I might be able to find a chink in Mr Cragthorne's armour after all.'

Dad held the front door and then followed me down the steps to the car. The cold made my back muscles clench and I was grateful for the ride. Dad whistled as he unlocked the car and slid into his seat.

'I don't get why you're so excited,' I said and fastened my seat belt. 'It'll be a petty vandalism charge at most. Hardly front-page news.'

'True, but a small crime can open the door for a bigger investigation. Your friend Benji might have paved the way for a huge prosecution.' Dad sighed happily as he pulled into traffic, ignoring the horn blaring behind us. 'And the headlines practically write themselves: GRAFFITI KID TAKES DOWN TYCOON! or REX CRAGTHORNE: SPRAY YOUR PRAYERS.'

Dad dropped me off across the street from the Beryl and fishtailed off in the direction of City Hall. He promised to let Linda know if he found anything she could use and asked me to give Della his love. I waved once, and then jogged across the street.

The Beryl was different.

It wasn't anything I could see, but there was the gentle hum of energy, like the happy drone of a beehive or a team before a big game. The atmosphere of unease that had hung over the building for the past week seemed to have lifted as the cast and crew bustled around getting things ready for dress rehearsal.

Jarvis and Pete were outside, replacing light bulbs on the marquee at the entrance to the theatre. They had the front door propped open and I slipped inside in time to run into Linda. She didn't even flinch; she had her phone pressed to her ear and a look of total satisfaction on her face.

'Well, tell him I have proof, and if he tries anything else, I'll know what to do with it.' She held up her hand, signalling me to wait.

Someone had been through the lobby with a broom and a mop and several extra tables were strategically laid out to hold drinks and hors d'oeuvres for the opening night party. Crisp white tablecloths matched the bare walls and made the room look like a modern art museum.

Linda ended the call with a satisfied swipe of her finger.

'I take it Benji's information helped?' I asked.

'You have no idea. I am going to enjoy introducing Rex

Cragthorne to our legal team.' Her eyes went distant and I could almost see the carnage she was imagining. Then she shook herself and came back the present. 'I've invited a small group of dedicated sponsors to attend the dress rehearsal. I should be back in time to greet them, but if you could let your mom know? They'll be here at five.'

'I'll tell her,' I agreed.

Linda nodded, a quick professional incline of her head. And then she skipped out the door like a school kid, ready to feed Rex Cragthorne to the sharks.

I hung my coat up in the cloakroom. Someone had moved the wooden coatrack out of the lobby. I guess it didn't fit the minimalist design.

I pushed my way through the lobby doors and into the theatre. Frank stood in front of the stage, arms crossed. Matthew Strange, Della and Vivian all stood on the stage.

'All right, and cue.' Frank's voice sounded weary, but there was an undercurrent of excitement to it. I shook my head. Theatre people lived for the thrill of being pushed to the edge and pulling the show together at the very last moment. If everything went smoothly, I think they'd be disappointed.

I watched for a few more minutes, then went to deliver Linda's message to my mom.

When I walked into the costume workshop, Mom looked up with a guilty start and threw a large sheet over her dressmaker's dummy. I caught a flash of electric-blue paisley cut close to the dress form. My outfit for opening night. I grimaced, hoping the deep-V neckline meant Mom hadn't finished sewing yet. I didn't complain, though. I'd already agreed to wear it. Mom would never let me back out now.

I spent the rest of the day helping where I was needed, double-checking props and costumes and laying programmes out for our honoured guests. Kevin showed up a little after lunch. He'd brought his *Zero Tolerance* DVD again, as well as a stack of shirts for Matthew Strange to sign.

The guests started arriving just before five.

Jarvis unlocked the front door at five o'clock sharp. A small group of people were already waiting outside and they hurried in to escape the cold. Jarvis stood there like a sentry, glaring at everyone. I almost expected him to start searching people's bags. Most of them were press, wearing their credentials around their necks. I recognized Gail Summers, the entertainment reporter from Dad's paper. Irinke and Ashley Barscay were there too. Irinke wore a dress of black sequins under her feathery coat and the replica of the Midnight Star around her neck.

Linda greeted Irinke like she was receiving the Queen, and paraded her in front of the press. Ashley lurked in the background.

'What is *he* doing here?' Kevin tugged on my arm and pointed towards the lobby door.

It was Benji.

I moved quickly. The last thing we needed was Benji making a scene in front of all those reporters. I grabbed the kid by the arm and marched him quickly out of sight.

'What do you think you're doing?' I asked when we were alone. He wasn't carrying a bag, but he was still wearing that puffy black coat. One pocket bulged suspiciously.

'Hey,' Benji said. 'That lady in the suit invited me.'

'Linda invited you?'

'Yeah. I'm all out of movie tickets, so I thought I'd give it a try.' He shrugged and looked around the theatre, sizing it up. He didn't look impressed.

'Oh, really,' I said. 'You didn't come here to vandalize the building?'

Benji shook his head and did his best to look innocent.

'Then what's that?' I poked a finger at Benji's side and felt metal through his coat.

'Hey!' Benji said, stepping back. 'That's my emergency can. I'm not going to use it, though, honest.'

I opened my mouth, but before I could speak, the lobby door swung open and Linda led her VIP audience into the theatre. She motioned for me to come over and say hello.

'Don't let him out of your sight,' I told Kevin. He nodded, cracked his knuckles and gave Benji his most winning smile. Benji grinned right back.

I spoke with Linda and her guests until the lights dimmed, then I took my seat next to Benji, blocking him in between me and Kevin. Benji hadn't tried anything, yet, but I wasn't taking any chances. The house lights dimmed and the low murmur of the audience died to silence. Benji put his feet up on the seat in front of him. The curtain rose and the play began.

As I watched the cast onstage, I was amazed what a difference lighting and costumes made. I'd only seen them rehearsing, and all the scenes I'd watched had been out of order. Now I felt like I was watching another world, not just a group of actors reading their lines.

I leant back in my chair and the thick red velvet scrunched beneath me. I had to admit, the show was pretty good. And from the eager silence of the audience, I wasn't the only one who thought so.

Vivian sat at her dressing table while Della helped arrange her hair. I blinked. It was the same scene Kevin and I had watched four days ago. Della and Vivian did their dance with the necklaces, Della offering pearls and Vivian demanding diamonds. I held my breath, but Matthew Strange made his cue this time, swinging his arm around like it had never been hurt. A small gasp of pleasure rippled through the audience at his appearance and I could see him biting the inside of his cheeks to keep the pleased smile off his face.

There was a sudden rasp, the sound of ripping fabric

and the *whoosh* of something heavy whistling through the air. The bottom of my stomach dropped and my knees turned to jelly as a large brown blur crashed into the stage.

CHAPTER

27

Sand sprayed everywhere.

My stomach lurched again. One of the sandbags had fallen, just like the one that had started the fire all the way back in 1927.

The audience erupted into sound. Reporters shouted questions and took pictures. The flashes were as dazzling as a lightning storm in the darkened room.

I raced down the aisle towards the stage, shouting for Kevin to stay with Benji. Vivian's scream made a tornado siren sound like a toy whistle. I looked up at the new chandelier for a moment, worried it might shatter.

Onstage, Matthew stood staring dumbfounded at the sagging pile of hessian at his feet, his mouth working open and closed like a goldfish. The sandbag had clipped the edge of the upper platform and taken a chunk of the railing with it before landing at his feet. Della made a sharp motion to someone in the wings and the curtain came rushing down.

I saw Linda climbing up on to the stage to address the crowd, but I didn't stop to hear what she was going to say. I vaulted past her and slid under the curtain. If someone had dropped that bag on purpose, I was going to find out who.

I ignored the cast and streaked across the stage. It was the fastest route to the ladder that led up on to the catwalk.

Jarvis stepped out of the wings, blocking my path. 'You should go back to your seat,' he said, his voice stern.

'You there, what's your name. Jasper. You're in charge of set safety, aren't you?' Matthew Strange strode across the stage. 'What is the meaning of this?'

I sprinted into the wings the second Jarvis was distracted.

The ladder was bolted too close to the wall and I scuffed my knuckles as I climbed. Eighteen rungs later I pulled myself on to the catwalk, a narrow walkway that stretched across the stage hidden from the audience by the top frill of the curtains.

I hadn't been fast enough. The catwalk was empty. If someone had dropped that sandbag on purpose, they were gone. Almost as if they'd vanished into thin air. I swallowed hard and shook the image of Kittie Grace's angry glare out of my head.

Below me, Vivian had stopped screaming and crumpled to the floor, her dress fanning around her in a giant circle of blue. The faint was no act this time. I swallowed hard. I shouldn't have looked down.

I pushed my way along the catwalk, holding tight to the railing and trying to will my knees to stop knocking. It was like being in the rigging of a giant boat. Ropes and pulleys criss-crossed through the Beryl's wooden scaffolding, and sandbags hung from the ropes like oversized sacks of flour.

I moved slowly towards the middle of the catwalk, checking the sandbags I could reach. Sandbags worked on a pulley system to help the crew pull heavy set pieces up into the empty fly space above the stage. If a set piece was down, the sandbag went up. And when the set went up, the sandbag came down.

I paused. The knots seemed . . . sloppy.

I gently pushed the nearest sandbag to one side, to see what was behind it. A wooden beam. Why would anyone untie a sandbag just to look at a wooden beam. I leant forward to get a closer look. There was a small hole in the wood. In fact, there were lots. A row of small wooden holes about the width of a pencil drew a line the entire length of the beam. They were fresh too, judging by the colour. I frowned and gently lowered the bag back into place.

In the middle of the catwalk, I found the loose end of a rope, dangling where the fallen sandbag should have hung. Its end was still sealed with wax – it hadn't been cut, or frayed with age. I was right. The knot hadn't been retied properly and it had given way.

I climbed back down to the stage into the middle of a hurricane. Vivian had recovered her voice and she was using it. Matthew was talking darkly into his mobile, while Frank flitted back and forth between the two stars like a butterfly having a panic attack.

Jarvis and Pete were frantically sweeping the stage, trying to get rid of the sand. And Della stared down at me giving me her very best *I told you so* look. The look was so good it took me a moment to notice she was trying not to shake.

I looked up at where my sister had been standing. Vivian hadn't been anywhere near where the bag hit the railing, but Della had. It had cracked the railing right next to the safe as Della switched out the necklaces. If it had been another few centimetres to the left . . . I shuddered and my skin went cold. The sandbag had almost hit Della.

'She wants to kill me,' Vivian shrieked, eyes so wide I could see white all the way around. 'Kittie Grace is trying to kill me.'

Matthew Strange glared after her. 'It almost hit *me* too, you know,' he yelled. I wanted to snap at both of them that they should stop worrying about themselves and start worrying about my sister, but Della caught my eye and shook her head.

Whatever force had been keeping Vivian together snapped. She screeched inartistically and sprinted from the stage, holding her hands over her head to ward off any other objects that might fly in her direction.

Frank ran after Vivian, and Della followed right behind him, treating me to one more helping of *I told you so* on her way offstage.

Matthew Strange stomped his foot. 'Fine. If anyone cares, I'll be in my dressing room.' He stalked offstage yelling, 'And will SOMEONE bring me a water.' Then he disappeared into the wings.

I stood alone in the middle of the stage. Pete and Jarvis had slipped away while Matthew Strange was making his grand exit. I could hear Linda on the other side of the curtain, trying to keep the audience under control. I shivered. I should have taken Della's concerns more seriously, but I had never thought some silly problems with a show could be so dangerous. I'd never forgive myself if something happened to Della and I could have stopped it.

I took a deep breath and peered up into the fly space above the stage. There was one good thing to come out of this disaster. Now I was certain the troubles inside the theatre weren't about ruining the show. Loosening the knots of the sandbag and hoping they fell at just the right time was no way to plan sabotage.

If someone had wanted a sandbag to ruin the show, they'd cut the rope themselves and make sure it did the job. But the holes in the beam? An original part of the Beryl? I finally understood. Someone was searching for a secret compartment. A compartment where a clever thief could have hidden the Midnight Star all the way back in 1927. It seemed like an odd place to search, but maybe they were running out of places to look.

But my new discovery didn't get me anywhere. I still had no idea how to catch the culprit. The knots could have been loosened days ago. I remembered the sand on the stage the night I'd almost fallen into the pit. It had probably happened then. It was just bad luck that the sandbag fell tonight.

Della came storming out of the wings. Her honey-blonde hair bobbing with each step, emphasizing just how serious this situation was.

'I told you this would happen,' she hissed, pulling me towards the wings. 'Come on. Matthew is sulking and Vivian's locked herself in her dressing room.'

'You want *me* to talk to her?'

'I want you to convince her there's no ghost out for her blood. Tell her about Rex Cragthorne and the sabotage.'

I opened my mouth and then quickly shut it again. It didn't seem like the right time to explain to Della that this wasn't sabotage – it was a careless treasure hunter. I stumbled slightly and caught myself.

How had the thief known to look for the necklace in the original parts of the theatre in the first place? All the stories I'd heard said the necklace had disappeared in the confusion after the fire. It wasn't until I'd read the original police files that I'd thought it might be possible that the necklace was hidden somewhere onstage.

I didn't have time to finish my train of thought. Della sped through the darkness with the sure feet of someone who's lived half of her life in the wings. I followed her blindly until we came through the door into the low amber light of backstage.

Frank and Mom stood outside Vivian's door. Frank had his mouth pressed against the wood and was speaking in soothing tones. Mom flashed us both concerned looks as we came round the corner.

'Any luck?' Della asked grimly.

Mom shook her head.

Frank knocked on the door again, wringing his hands. He kept glancing over his shoulder and I realized he had another star throwing a tantrum as well.

'You go deal with Matthew,' Mom said. 'He'll be easier to handle than her.'

'You'd better bring him a water as well,' I said, remembering Matthew's exiting line.

Frank threw up his hands and spun on his heel, disappearing down the hall to Matthew's dressing room. 'Prima donnas, I'm surrounded by prima donnas.'

'Della, I thought I told you to go lie down,' Mom said as she knocked on Vivian's door again. 'Come on, Vivian, the show must go on.'

'I won't!'

Mom sighed and turned back to Della. 'Use the spare dressing room. You've had a shock too.'

Della shook her head. 'I'm fine. Besides, that place is filthy. I couldn't relax if I tried.'

Mom didn't look convinced. She gave me a pleading look. I could have told her Della was tougher than that, but then I had a better idea.

'I'll sit with her,' I said, and grabbed Della's wrist before she could protest. Mom smiled at me gratefully and I pulled Della down the corridor into the dressing room next door.

'I can't rest now, Alice.' Della twisted her wrist free and glared at me. 'We need to get Vivian to finish the dress rehearsal. You need to explain it to her. If you can show her the facts—'

'It won't make any difference,' I said. 'You saw her, she's so freaked out she wouldn't listen to reason if it bit her on the nose.'

'So what, you're just going to give up?'

'No,' I said with thin smile. 'We're going to fight fire with fire.'

I pointed up at the vent that shared the wall with Vivian's dressing room. Della followed my finger and then she looked at me, confused.

'How good is your ghostly apparition voice?' I asked.

'Passable,' Della said slowly, her eyes widening in comprehension. 'But what should I say? Even if I pretend to be Kittie Grace, she's not going to believe me if I just say I'm not trying to kill her.'

'I don't know, you're the dramatic one. Tell her you want her to have the part and someone else is trying to stop the show. Tell her there's an evil spirit and only performing *The Curse of the Casterfields* can save the day. Tell her the show must go on.'

Della nodded. She closed her eyes and her face went blank as she got into character, and when she opened her eyes they were wild and haunted. She glanced around the room like it might close in on her at any moment.

'Got it?' I asked.

Della nodded.

I dragged a large steamer trunk underneath the vent and held Della's hand as she climbed on top of it, bringing her eyes level with the vent.

And then I left my sister to scare Vivian Rollins back onstage.

CHAPTER

28

I walked out of the dressing room and ran into Kevin. He must have managed to slip past Jarvis in the confusion.

'Is everyone OK?' Kevin asked.

I nodded. 'Della's pretty shaken up, and Vivian's locked herself in her dressing room, but no one got hurt.'

'What about Matthew Strange?'

'He's fine too.'

'Phew, that's good.'

I didn't respond. It wasn't good. It was lucky. That sand-bag had almost hit Della. It was one thing when it was just messing around with props and searching dressing rooms, but whoever was looking for the Midnight Star had gone too far. They needed to be stopped. The problem was, I still had no idea who the culprit was.

I scowled. I needed my notes. There had to be a clue,

234

something I'd missed. Some detail I'd overlooked that would make the whole equation fall into place.

'Where are we going?' Kevin asked as he followed me through the backstage corridors. I could hear the low murmur of the journalists and other guest as we passed the lobby. Linda must have moved them in there to enjoy the snacks and drinks that were meant for intermission.

I stopped suddenly and whirled around to face him. 'Where's Benji?'

Kevin shrugged. 'He thought the pyrotechnics were cool, so I introduced him to Pete.'

I took a few deep breaths and told my shoulders to stop hanging out with my ears, then I kept walking. I didn't have time to worry about Benji and explosions.

I'd left my things in the costume workshop, the cloak-room being reserved for the VIPs. I grabbed my bag and turned it upside down. A black and white snowfall of paper blanketed the floor. I knelt down beside it, spreading the pages out as if that would help me see the whole picture. Now that I knew the motive was finding the Star, maybe I'd see something I'd missed before.

I scanned the pages desperately, waiting for the pieces to start falling into place. They didn't. It didn't matter that the motive was different. I still had the same problem, the equation had too many variables. All the incidents happened late at night, or at a time that was impossible to pin down.

I practically growled in frustration. 'It just doesn't add up,' I said, and flopped back against the wall.

Kevin sat down on the floor next to me. 'Maybe you should try working backwards.'

I looked up at him blankly. 'What?'

'That's what you told me to do when I couldn't solve a problem. I mean, you know what the bad guy is after, so maybe it would be easier to just find that.'

I snorted. 'The Midnight Star isn't here,' I said. 'They just think it is. How am I supposed to find something that doesn't exist?'

And then it hit me. I didn't need to find the real necklace. Just like Della and Vivian and the ghost, just like the lobby display, all I needed to do was tell them a story they wanted to believe.

'Where's Benji?' I asked.

Kevin looked at me like I'd finally lost it.

'There isn't time to explain. Just get him and meet me back here.'

Kevin raised an eyebrow at me.

'And tell him to bring his spray paint.'

I found one of the five fake Midnight Stars in Linda's desk in the theatre office. It was heavy and cold and sparkled in my hand. I wondered, for a moment, what made the real Midnight Star different. I mean, a diamond is just a really dense lump of coal. What's so great about that? Besides if no one knew the jewels were fake, did it even matter? I slipped the necklace into my pocket and snuck back to where Kevin and Benji were waiting in the costume workshop.

Della's spooky voice must have worked, because dress rehearsal was back on track. The Beryl was filled with the electric tension of a live performance. Linda's drinks and snacks must have helped too. Every now and again, I could hear the muffled sound of the audience laughing and gasping in all the right spots.

Benji sat on the couch with his arms crossed. 'You want me to what?'

'I want you to show me how your booby trap worked. Show me how to set it up.'

'No way, that is need-to-know information and you do not need to know. I can't believe you're making me miss the ending. Pete said there's an epic explosion.'

I gritted my teeth. Kevin stood up and glared down at Benji. Benji didn't even flinch.

'Look,' I said. 'If you help me out tonight, I'll get you tickets for tomorrow. There's going to be a party, and lots of free food,' I added quickly, to sweeten the deal.

Benji tipped his head to the side, thinking it over.

'And,' I said, 'if this works, you'll have helped catch a dangerous criminal.'

Benji nodded appreciatively. 'Fine, I'll show you how it works, and I'll give you the can. But if we get a reward,

I want half.'

'Fine,' I agreed quickly. Fifty per cent of zero was still zero.

Benji ran me through the basics of booby-trapping a spray can and then hurried back to his seat. I guess he really didn't want to miss that last explosion. Which, given Benji's love of booby traps, was a little worrying. I hoped Pete wasn't trusting enough to let the kid have any flash powder of his own.

I looked at the clock. Thirty minutes until the curtain came down. I worked quickly, prepping Benji's emergency can with strong black thread from my mom's sewing box and some supplies from Pete's toolbox. Kevin stood guard at the door.

'Are you sure this is a good idea?' he asked.

I shrugged. 'Not really, but it's the best thing I can come up with. We're lucky that sandbag didn't kill someone. Who knows what else might happen if we don't put a stop to it now.'

'OK,' Kevin said slowly. 'But once you hide the necklace and set up the trap, how is the thief going to know about it?'

I finished stringing the thread through the can and hid it inside my shirt.

'After dress rehearsal, there's always a small party. Everyone who's had access to the Beryl for the past few weeks will be there. All we need to do is let a few people overhear that I found the trapdoor and the room underneath when the sandbag hit the stage. If we make everyone think the builders are coming in the morning to seal it up, then the thief will have to search there tonight.'

Kevin looked sceptical. 'Are you sure?'

'Gossip spreads like wildfire backstage. Trust me, the thief will get the message.'

'If you say so.'

'I do,' I said. And tried my best to sound like I meant it.

CHAPTER

29

'This is insane,' Della said as she crouched in the sooty darkness beside me. 'Do you really think this will work?'

I'd had to tell Della about the plan because I needed her to help spread the rumour. And once Della knew we were staking out the stage, there was no getting rid of her. She told Mom she was sleeping over with me and Dad. I felt horrible for lying, but it was the only way.

We'd hidden up on the catwalk until everyone else had gone home. I'd set up the trap as quickly as possible and then the three of us took up our position in the wings to wait and watch in silence. Or we should have. Della kept asking questions. She always talked a blue streak when she was nervous. I turned to her and tried to keep my voice level.

'Whoever wants the Midnight Star is desperate. They won't take the risk that one of the builders might find it.'

'And you're sure it's a person and not a ghost?' Della asked, her voice a whisper.

I rolled my eyes in the darkness. 'Very sure,' I said. 'Now keep quiet.'

Minutes ticked by. Nothing happened.

Onstage the ghost light shone, its soft light making the shadows around the stage even darker. I crouched on my heels, ready to stand up and make a run for it when the culprit came in. The idea wasn't to catch them red-handed. I wasn't that reckless. The idea was for the paint to leave its mark, the way a dye pack marks a bank robber.

Time stretched out and every shift and creak of the ancient building sent my heart racing. Kevin fidgeted with the toggles on his coat, clicking them against each other until I elbowed him into silence.

Nothing.

And then, I heard it. The unmistakable sound of foot-steps. They were coming from the other side of the stage. I strained my eyes in the darkness. A figure stepped out of the wings across from us. I couldn't tell who it was since he wore all black, a cap pulled low over his head. The ghost light cast his long shadow down the stage and threw his profile into darkness as he opened the trapdoor and dropped inside.

Kevin tensed like he was getting ready to spring and I

grabbed his arm. We needed to wait. There was no point in setting a trap if we didn't let the culprit spring it.

'Wait for it,' I said under my breath and started counting primes. My hand was sweating and the heavy metal handle of the torch slipped against my palm.

Two, three, five, seven, eleven, thirteen . . .

There was a yelp of shocked surprise followed by spluttering coughs and a low hissing sound. Benji's trap had hit home.

'Now?' Kevin asked.

'Now,' I said, and we rushed on to the stage.

Della and I pointed our torches into the hole and Kevin held his phone ready.

'Come out now,' I said, and hoped I sounded more confident than I felt.

A large round face stained deepest indigo blinked into the beam of my torch. He raised his hand to shield his eyes and the Midnight Star flashed between his fingers.

'Pete?' I couldn't believe it. 'It was you?'

Pete blinked a few times, still disoriented from finding a spring-loaded can of spray paint along with the Midnight Star. 'What's going on?' he asked, blinking at the bright light.

I sighed and clicked it off. 'Pete, I know you've been looking for the Star. You've been scaring everyone sense-less. You almost killed my sister.'

'What!' Pete's voice snapped out in disbelief.

'You moved the sandbags so you could drill holes in the scaffolding, but you didn't tie them properly when you put them back.' Even as I said it, it sounded wrong.

Pete's already wide eyes opened even further. 'Drilling holes in the scaffolding? I would never do something so dangerous. And I never moved the sandbags, and even if I did I can tie a sandbag off blindfolded with my hands behind my back.'

I crossed my arms. 'If it wasn't you, then why are you here?'

I couldn't see it because of the paint, but I think Pete blushed.

'When I heard Della say you'd found a secret room under the stage I thought I'd just come look. If we found the Star we could sell it to raise money for the Beryl. And maybe poor Mr Oswald's ghost could finally be put to rest.'

Della gasped. 'You think the ghost is Oswald?'

'Who else would it be?'

Della nodded thoughtfully. I put my head in my hands. That was just like Pete. He wouldn't hurt the Beryl, plus as an experienced stagehand he'd know all sorts of complicated knots for making the rigging secure. The knots I'd seen on the sandbags looked like they'd been tied by a kindergarten student.

'Um, Alice?' Kevin said, tugging on the hem of my shirt.

I narrowed my eyes at Pete, just because I didn't like it didn't mean he wasn't the one behind the trouble. I opened my mouth.

Kevin tugged harder. 'Alice,' he hissed. 'Listen.'

Something in Kevin's tone made me stop. I tilted my head to one side and listened. Footsteps. Coming from the direction of the Stage Door. Coming closer.

'Pete,' I whispered. 'Did you bring someone with you?'

He shook his head.

The door between the hall and the wings clicked as someone turned the knob.

'Quick,' I said. 'Hide.'

I pushed Kevin and Della towards the hole. Pete scrambled awkwardly out of their way, hunching over to avoid the low ceiling. I jumped in after them, grabbing the edge of the trapdoor as I fell and pulling it shut behind me.

Darkness swallowed us.

Pete started to say something.

'Shhh,' I said.

'What are we doing?' Kevin whispered, his breath hot against my temple. My mind raced as I tried to figure out what to do. If the real thief was still out there and worked out this was a trap, they might stop looking for the necklace. That would be good for the Beryl, but I didn't know if I'd ever be happy if I didn't know who was really behind all the troubles.

'Pete sprung the trap,' I said. 'The only way we can stop the thief now is to catch him red-handed.'

Pete didn't say a word as he tried to wrap his brain

about just what he'd walked into.

The darkness beneath the stage was so complete that specks of imaginary light started to flash and swirl in my vision, as if my eyes were trying to fill the darkness all by themselves. I flicked on my torch and found my way to the control panel.

I grabbed the spray-paint can and put it gently on the floor. It would only give the trap away. Then I shoved the fake necklace back into its hiding place and shut the compartment door.

The stage creaked above us. There was something a little heavier about the sound, more solid, and then it creaked again. I hurried across the small space, shoving Pete, Della and Kevin into the far corner, and turned off the light.

I held my breath as I listened to the footsteps overhead.

The trapdoor screeched and a slightly lighter shade of black opened up in the ceiling above us. I pressed further into the corner of the room, trying to melt into the shadows.

There was a moment of total silence and then a dull thump as someone dropped into the hole. The sound was soft, like whoever jumped in had experience falling into small dark spaces.

A small penlight flicked on, and I flinched, afraid we'd been caught, but the light wasn't pointing in our direction. It swept over the wall and found the closed door of the control panel and stopped.

The backwash of the light reflected on a figure dressed all in black, medium height and build. He had the slow stealth of a snake, and moved towards the panel without making a sound. A black knitted cap hid any trace of hair. I noticed a string tied around the back of the cap and realized that whoever it was was wearing a mask.

I spread my arms, holding everyone back. We'd already had one false alarm, and this time there was no can of paint to mark the criminal. I needed him to take the fake Midnight Star, and I needed a picture of him doing it. At least this time I knew we had the right person. No one innocent sneaks into a building at night wearing all black and a mask. I held up my phone and then I gave a silent groan.

What good was a picture if the criminal was wearing a mask?

Sure, maybe the police could do some fancy ear recognition or something, but I wasn't the police. I needed a face. My mind raced. I only had a few seconds before the thief had the necklace and left. If I didn't act fast he'd get away.

I handed Kevin my phone and motioned to him to stay put, to take the picture. Then I pointed at myself, the thief and my face. I was starting to wish I'd taken that mime class with Della, but Kevin seemed to understand and I didn't have time to waste making sure.

The thief already had the panel open and was rooting

around inside. There was a small hiss of excitement as his penlight flashed against the jewels. It was now or never.

'Stop!' I shouted, and turned on my torch, pointing it at the thief.

The figure froze, penlight clutched between his teeth and the fake Midnight Star dangling from his hand. Out of the corner of my eye, I could see movement in the darkness – Kevin or Della, moving into position. I kept my eyes locked on the thief, careful not to let my gaze give them away. I just needed to keep his attention for a few more minutes.

The thief made a small hiccoughing sound of surprise. It wasn't the kind of sound I expected from a masked intruder. He paused for a minute, gathering himself, and then dropped the necklace into a pouch that hung around his neck. He took a step backwards, towards the trapdoor.

'I said, stop. That belongs to the Beryl.'

The thief didn't listen. He reached up and grabbed on to the edge of the stage and pulled up with the strength and grace of a gymnast.

I had to stop him.

'Alice, no!' Della shouted, but I didn't listen.

I jumped forward and grabbed on to the figure's legs. I didn't care how strong he was, there was no way he could pull me up as well. He tried to kick his legs free, but I held on for dear life. The struggle didn't last long. It didn't need to. After half a second, Pete stepped forward and yanked on the thief's shirt, pulling him down. We landed in an undignified lump on the floor.

The thief kicked and wriggled, trying to untangle himself from my legs. He must have thought I was going to keep trying to hold him, but I wasn't that crazy. I let him slip free, stretched up my arms and dragged the mask from his face.

I heard the snap of a camera shutter.

It was Ashley Barscay.

CHAPTER 30

Pete looked at Ashley for a second. And then he sat on him.

The breath escaped from Ashley's lungs in a giant whoosh and the fight went with it.

'Della,' Pete said, his voice very steady. 'Can you get me some rope from backstage? And after that, please call the police.'

Della nodded and scrambled out of the trapdoor. Her footsteps disappeared towards the wings overhead.

I took a good look at Ashley. It hadn't occurred to me that the thief might be someone who wasn't part of the cast or crew, but when I thought about it, Ashley and Irinke were around the Beryl more than I was. I remembered how much Ashley knew about diamonds. I'd thought it was because Irinke was his aunt, but maybe there was more to it than that. I wondered if he'd stolen things from her too.

My eyes widened. Ashley had been with Irinke at the charity ball the night the Astor cousin's sapphires had been stolen. He'd even been talking to her. I wondered how many parties he got to go to as Irinke's escort, and how many jewels went missing when he was around. It was him – *he* was the thief who Interpol was after.

I took the pouch from around Ashley's neck, opening it and pulling out the fake Midnight Star. Ashley bared his teeth at me, but didn't say a word. I kept looking and found a small stack of silver calling cards.

I took one out and held it under the torch. It was printed in silver ink, only slightly darker than the card itself and I had to squint to make out the words in the low light.

The Phantom.

I took a step back and stared at Ashley, and then at the cards.

I walked slowly back to the metal door where I'd hidden the necklace. One of the cards rested there in place of the necklace.

'You leave a calling card?' I asked, picking it up. 'Isn't that a little bit cheesy?' I smiled. Dad was going to have a field day with this one.

And then the ghost light went out.

The steady glow of warm yellow light that had been filtering in through the trapdoor vanished and my torch barely cut through the gloom.

'Della?' I called, suddenly aware that my sister had been gone an awfully long time.

Silence.

I swept my torch over the room. Pete still had Ashley pinned to the floor. But the corners of the Phantom's mouth were tucked up into a smirk. I flicked the torch a little further. Kevin was still there too.

'Stay here,' I said softly. 'I'm going to go see if I can find Della.'

I took a deep careful breath and reminded myself that there are no such things as ghosts. Then I went back to the trapdoor and pulled myself on to the stage. I wasn't half as strong as Ashley or nearly as graceful, but after a few kicks and a helpful shove from Kevin, I made it out.

The stage was pitch-black. I swept my torch around, trying to orient myself. The beam rippled over an odd lump and I turned back. It was Della.

I rushed across the stage. Someone had tied my sister to the set staircase and stuffed a large square of black cloth into her mouth. My heart leapt up into my throat. I pulled the cloth free. Della's eyes were wide and terrified.

'What happened?' I asked as I fumbled at the knots.

'Look out,' Della hissed. I felt the air rush behind me and I rolled to the side, fighting to get my fear under control.

A painfully thin figure dressed all in black darted out of the shadows, rolling past me and snatching the Phantom card from my hand. He was smooth and fast and made Ashley look like a three-footed sloth.

I whirled round, willing myself to see in the dark. Ashley must have had a partner.

I back-pedalled towards the front of the stage, trying to keep my movements random and unpredictable. I'd dropped my torch when I rolled, but there was no point trying to retrieve it. Holding a light in a dark room would paint a target on my back. But I couldn't keep running for ever. If I wanted to catch the other Phantom, I needed to think of a plan. And fast.

My heel hit the edge of the stage and I stopped cold, swallowing hard. One more step and I would have fallen backwards into the orchestra pit. I closed my eyes, it was a gamble, but it was probably the best chance I was going to get.

I took a breath and then I shouted, 'Kevin! Get help. I'll keep him busy! I'll keep the necklace safe.'

My voice gave my position away as clearly as a spotlight. I could hear Kevin under the stage, running across the floor towards the second exit. The Phantom could only chase one of us. I crossed my fingers he would choose me and dropped silently to my belly. It worked. As soon as my cheek touched the stage I felt the air move above my head as the Phantom dived forward, rushing towards the last place from where he'd heard my voice.

I didn't wait for the crash or the shouts of pain when

he hit the bottom of the pit. I just got up and ran, through the wings and up the small hallway. I burst out into the theatre and began running towards the lobby. Kevin could only get out by the Stage Door and I needed to keep the Phantom as far away from there as possible.

I slowed down. Listened for footsteps. The theatre was silent. I licked my lips. Mom was going to kill me.

'You won't get away with this,' I shouted into the darkness. 'I know who you are.'

There was a hiss of sound to my left and I took a quick step back, pressing into the lobby door. My mind raced furiously. If Ashley was only half of the Phantom, there was only one person his partner could be.

'Irinke Barscay. I know it's you. I know you're Ashley's partner.'

The hiss turned into a dry, papery sound and I realized the Phantom was laughing. And she was right in front of me!

I leant back against the lobby door and pushed. The door swung open and a slice of orange street light streaked into the theatre, illuminating a figure all in black. She wore the same type of mask as Ashley.

'Partner. Ha.' She spat out the words. The fabric of the mask distorted her voice, but now that I knew it was Irinke I could recognize it. 'Don't make me laugh. My turnip of an apprentice has been trying to usurp me. As if *he* could be the Phantom.'

Irinke took a step closer and I mirrored her, backing into the lobby. I didn't know how long it would take Kevin to get help. All I knew was I needed to keep stalling.

'Ashley's your apprentice?' I asked, edging backwards. If I could get her into the lobby, I might be able to trick her into the cloakroom and lock the door until the police arrived. It wasn't the best plan I'd ever come up with, but it was better than nothing.

Irinke snorted. 'The most useless apprentice I've ever trained. Greedy and impatient, always stealing when he should be waiting, and waiting when he should act.'

'So it wasn't you at the Liberty Ball? You didn't steal the sapphires.'

'Of course not. I'm a professional. I was only here for the real prize. The Midnight Star. But Ashley sees something shiny and he takes it, like a child. He leaves those dreadful cards, as if a good thief wants fame. If I hadn't promised his mother on her deathbed that I would look after him . . .' Irinke's voice died away and she looked at me suspiciously. Like I'd been the one making her talk.

I took another step back.

'It doesn't matter,' Irinke said. 'He's gone too far. He tried to steal the Star from me. The police can have him.'

I shuffled backwards towards the cloakroom. I could see Irinke's smile grow as she watched me – she thought she was backing me into a corner. To be fair, she was right.

'Why are you telling me all this?'

'Why not? No one will ever believe you. They never believe children, no matter how smart they are. And you are smart, aren't you?' Irinke took a deep breath and her voice became almost wistful. It made my skin crawl. 'If circumstances were different, I could have trained you to be a wonderful thief.' She stepped through the door into the cloakroom. 'Now give me the Star, so I don't have to hurt you.'

'I don't have it,' I said, pressing back against the wall.

Irinke hissed. 'Don't play games. I can see it in your hand.'

She moved forward slowly, stalking across the room. I took a deep breath and tried to regulate my breathing. Just a few more steps and I'd have space to run around her.

'This isn't the real Star. It's a fake.'

'What?' I practically expected a forked tongue to dart between her lips.

'The necklace, it's a fake. I hid it under the stage to trick you.'

She eyed me suspiciously but didn't take another step. I swallowed hard. It was now or never.

'See for yourself,' I said, and I tossed the Midnight Star into the air. It arced up in a high parabola, Irinke had to step forward to catch the necklace as it fell, and as soon as she moved, I ran.

I didn't get far.

She was fast for an older woman. Her years of experience as a dancer had left her strong and lithe. Irinke jumped, snatched the Midnight Star from mid-air and spun in one smooth motion, grabbing the back of my shirt and dragging me to the floor before I got more than a step past her.

I hit the floor with a thud and tried to scramble to my feet.

It was no use. Irinke planted a foot firmly on my chest. 'Stay,' she said, and pressed down hard enough to make my lungs hurt. She held up the Midnight Star uncertainly. She glared at me, and then brought the necklace up to her lips and touched the enormous diamond gently to the tip of her tongue. Her eyes flashed. 'Where is the real one?'

I shrugged. 'I don't know. Someone stole it, someone found it, or it was lost in the fire. It could be anywhere.'

'But the police files . . . it has to be here. You're hiding it! Give it to me!' Irinke pressed her foot harder into my chest, squeezing the air out of my lungs one breath at a time.

'I don't know,' I gasped, but Irinke didn't believe me.

I felt the last puff of air leaving my lungs. My head felt as heavy as lead and my ears rang. Blood hammered inside my head like a drum solo, or maybe it was more like the sound of running feet. I tried to twist to one side, but it was no use, I didn't have the strength. I was drowning in sand and no one was going to save me.

Darkness closed around me like a tunnel.

And then there was light. Blinding electric light.

The weight lifted off my chest suddenly and I gasped in air like it was going out of style. I blinked and coughed and the room swam back into focus. Kevin was helping me sit up. Della watched from the doorway, her face very pale.

Irinke Barscay lay sprawled on the floor, her hands pinned behind her back and Jarvis knelt on top of her. I blinked again. For a second I thought he was fastening a jewelled bracelet around her wrist. My eyes focused and I realized it was a pair of handcuffs.

'Irinke Barscay, you are under arrest for burglary, grand larceny' – he spoke like he was reading a script, then he looked over at me – 'and assault.'

CHAPTER 31

I sat in the costume workshop, a rough grey blanket wrapped around my shoulders. Della and Kevin sat on either side of me, sporting grey blankets of their own. The police had showed up a few minutes after Jarvis snapped the cuffs on Irinke Barscay.

Pete had sat on Ashley the whole time. The apprentice Phantom looked almost relieved to be in handcuffs when they led him away.

The Beryl buzzed with official police activity. I wanted to call Dad, he'd give an arm for an inside scoop like this. But when I took out my phone, Jarvis snatched it before I could dial. I guess he didn't want me to alert the media just yet.

Someone handed me a cup of coffee from the 7-Eleven and I looked up, startled to see the suspicious clerk. He wore his usual black pants and green polo shirt, but now there was a gold badge hanging from a lanyard around his neck. A badge with a government logo on it.

He gave me a small smile, looked down at the badge and shrugged, then went back to supervising the small team of cops who were processing evidence. I sipped my coffee and tried not to stare too hard. I guess that explained why he was so suspicious of everyone. It was a job requirement.

The man in charge of everyone was Jarvis. Or, I guess, Agent Jarvis. He'd put on a navy blue windbreaker with official patches on the shoulders and INTERPOL stencilled on the back in blocky white letters. He wore a matching baseball cap as well, and also had a gold badge clipped to his belt. He was in the middle of a phone call, but waved when he saw me looking.

I waved back.

Mom and Linda came rushing in a few minutes later. One of the police must have called them. There are rules against talking to minors without an adult present.

'Alice, Della, are you OK?' Mom fell to her knees in front of the couch and wrapped us both in a spine-crushing hug. I held my coffee cup out to one side and tried not to let too much slosh over the brim.

'I'm fine, Mom,' Della said, her eyes aglow. I could almost see her reliving the experience, searing each new emotion into her memory for future use in case she ever got cast as a damsel in distress. Mom nodded once, then turned to me.

I swallowed. Hard. Next to me, Kevin tried to turn himself invisible.

But instead of lecturing, Mom just crushed me against her in another enormous hug. 'Alice Jones, what am I going to do with you?' she said, her voice muffled in my hair. 'I'd tell you never to do something like that again, but I have a feeling you wouldn't listen to me anyway.'

'I'm sorry, Mom, I just—'

'I know, I know, you just can't leave something unfinished. And you got your father's sense of justice too. I understand.'

'I thought it was just someone messing around looking for the necklace. I didn't think it would be the Phantom.'

She looked up at the ceiling and back at me. 'I can't believe I'm saying this. Next time I won't tell you not to investigate *but*, if you're going to do something risky, you need to tell me. I may not be able to stop you and your gigantic brain, but I can help keep you safe.'

I blinked, stunned, and then nodded. I could live with that.

'OK, good. I need to go sign some release forms so I can take you home. I called your dad, and he'll be waiting to hear all the details. Kevin, your mom is on her way too.'

Mom brushed back a loose strand of hair, then stood, tugged her shirt into place and went to go talk to Agent

7–Eleven. Della went with her, still clutching the grey blanket around her shoulders.

Kevin's mom showed up in record time. She wore a bathrobe and curlers and an expression like a dragon getting ready to lay waste to a village. Kevin didn't seem too worried, though. He stood up and handed me his blanket.

'Are you going to be OK?' I asked.

Kevin shot me his trademark angel smile. 'Are you kidding? I'm gonna be fine, I'm a hero.'

I laughed, then stopped when I saw his mom eyeballing us from across the room.

'What time should I pick you up for the show tomorrow?' Kevin asked.

I quailed before his mom's epically raised eyebrow. 'How about I meet you here?'

'Suit yourself,' he said with a smile and headed off to charm the dragon.

Agent Jarvis finished his call with a satisfied grunt and tucked his phone into the case clipped to his belt. He dragged a metal folding chair across the room and sat down across from me.

'So you're the agent with Interpol,' I said.

Agent Jarvis looked up, a sharp little motion full of surprise.

'My dad's a crime reporter with the *Philadelphia Daily News*. He's been trying to get an interview,' I explained, before his surprise grew into suspicion.

I watched as the blank expression softened, and then a new understanding dawned. 'Arthur Jones is your father.' He chuckled ruefully. 'I've been dodging him for days now. I couldn't blow my cover.'

'I know.'

Jarvis raised an eyebrow at me and I grinned.

'But why were you here?' I asked. 'Why didn't you stake out the parties?'

'We got a tip that the Phantom was going after the Midnight Star.'

I remembered Irinke's disdain for her useless apprentice and his ambitions to be the new Phantom. Ashley might have wanted her to get arrested. It didn't seem very smart to try to steal the Star himself after he warned the cops, but maybe he didn't think they'd listened. Jarvis had fooled me. I had no idea he was undercover.

'When we got the report about the theft at the Liberty Ball I was worried that we'd been duped. Those sapphires were nowhere near the calibre the Phantom usually stole.'

'That was Ashley,' I said slowly.

Agent Jarvis raised his eyebrows even higher.

'Irinke's apprentice. Not a very good one, she said. He had impulse control issues.'

'Ah.' Jarvis leant back in his chair. 'That explains the mess he made trying to find the necklace for himself. We've been after the real Phantom for decades and she's never been so sloppy. I thought she was losing her touch.'

'What I don't understand, though,' I said slowly, 'is why Irinke thought the Midnight Star was here in the first place. And why did she go after it now? She could have stolen it years ago.'

'Think about it. What's different about the Beryl now?' Jarvis smiled at me and his eyes flashed with hidden intelligence.

I suddenly realized I was talking to a real live detective. I frowned, thinking furiously. I didn't want him to tell me the answer, I wanted to work it out for myself.

'Rex Cragthorne!' I practically shouted.

Linda looked up sharply and stared at me from across the room. Jarvis's smile deepened.

'Rex Cragthorne tried to buy the building and have it demolished. If he succeeded, the Midnight Star would be gone for ever. And if the Beryl became a success again, the necklace would probably be found during the restoration.'

'Exactly. And in order to get access to the theatre . . .' Jarvis trailed off, waiting for me to connect the dots.

'Irinke became a patron of the arts. That's why she donated all that money to the Beryl. So she could have access.'

Linda made a small strangled sound, and the colour drained out of her face. 'The money Irinke donated was all stolen?'

Agent Jarvis tilted his head from side to side. 'Not

exactly. But much of it is proceeds from crime. I'm afraid the Beryl's assets may have to be frozen while we sort out the details.'

'But . . . you can't. Tomorrow is opening night.'

Agent Jarvis stood up. 'You should be grateful. If we thought you knew about who Irinke was, you'd be in more than just financial trouble.'

Linda closed her mouth with an abrupt snap and gave Jarvis a shrewd look. 'I should have known your references were too good to be true.'

Jarvis shrugged. 'I needed to get the job.'

Linda looked from Agent Jarvis to me and then sank on to the couch and let her head fall into her hands. 'Oh, Alice,' she said. 'If only you'd found the real Midnight Star.'

'I wouldn't worry too much, Linda,' Jarvis said, his voice more gentle than before. 'I'll have a word and make sure any money that didn't come from Irinke is free for you to use.'

Linda looked up thoughtfully.

'Besides, think of all the publicity you'll get. People have been trying to catch the Phantom for decades.'

Linda paused. 'You're right,' she said, her publicity wheels spinning like crazy. 'I need to make some calls.'

Agent Jarvis watched her walk away and then turned to me. 'Well, my work here is done. I like to think I'd have caught the Phantom eventually, but thank you for your help.' He handed me a business card. 'If there's ever anything I can do to repay the favour, don't hesitate to call.'

I looked at the card. I could feel a smile spreading across my face.

'There is one thing you could do . . .' I said.

I sat in the front as Mom drove me home. Della lay in the back. She'd fallen asleep before we'd reached the end of the block.

We drove in silence, but it wasn't uncomfortable. The snowy streets were quiet and still.

'I'm sorry things went so bad tonight,' I said.

Mom giggled.

'What?'

'You know what they say. The worse the dress rehearsal the better the show. After tonight, we'll all win Tonys.'

We laughed until we cried.

Mom pulled up on Passfield Avenue. I could tell Dad was home because the Plymouth was parked in front of the house, one wheel on the kerb, the back bumper jutting into the street. Mom saw it too, and shook her head. I climbed out of the car before she could say anything.

'Alice, wait,' Mom said. 'Here.' She reached behind her and pulled out a large grey garment bag. 'I finished your outfit for the party tomorrow.'

I felt my stomach sink, but didn't let it show on my face. Mom had worked hard to finish it in time, so the least I could do was wear her dress for one night. Especially after all the trouble I'd just put her through.

'Thanks, Mom,' I said, and tried to sound like I meant it. And maybe I did, just a little bit. At least now I didn't have to pick something out for myself. I waved goodbye and climbed the concrete steps to the front door, my smile growing wider with each step as I figured out the best way to tell Dad I'd just gotten him an exclusive interview with Interpol.

CHAPTER

32

I stood in my room and stared at the garment bag hanging on the back of my closet. My wet hair cooling quickly, I shivered, mostly because of the cold. I'd been putting off opening the bag. I knew wearing the dress Mom made me would make her happy, but the thought of it made my teeth ache.

Downstairs, Dad was madly typing up his story before we had to go. He'd gotten the call from Agent Jarvis that morning and locked himself in his office. I'd spent the day reading *Fermat's Last Theorem*. Or trying to. I still couldn't stop thinking about the Midnight Star. The Phantom was no fool, so something must have made her think the necklace was still at the Beryl to go to all that trouble. I shook my head. I was stalling and I knew it.

I took a deep breath and stepped forward, opening the

bag with one strong tug of the zipper.

I expected an explosion of tulle or satin in bright peacock blue. But nothing popped out. I peeled back the side of the bag and blinked. Charcoal-grey trousers, a tailored jacket and a soft white shirt made of silk. Not a dress, a suit.

I opened the front of the jacket, and smiled. It had peacock-blue paisley lining. Something warm sparked inside my chest and my vision blurred for a moment. I blinked the suit back into focus and then I stopped wasting time and got dressed.

'Dad, we need to go!' I pounded on the door to his office. It was 6.27 a.m. I heard his typing shift into warp speed.

'Just a minute.'

Two more minutes of furious typing and the unmistakable click of the mouse as he emailed it to his editor and I stepped away from the door just in time for Dad to swing it open.

I raised my eyebrows.

'Hey, I've got the tux until Sunday, I might as well make the most of it?' he said with a smile.

With Dad driving, we made it to the Beryl in plenty of time.

When we got to the lobby, I almost didn't recognize it. The doors were open and the lobby was full of people all dressed to the nines. It was wall-to-wall tuxedos and ballgowns. I looked down at myself and felt a little happy that I wasn't wearing my usual jeans with the ragged hems. Everyone was talking and drinking champagne and looking at the lobby display with great interest.

Most of the crowd was gathered around the replica Midnight Star in the middle of the room, oohing and aahing and taking pictures. But there was a lot of interest in Pete's limelight as well. Even the old vitrified sandbag and my card explaining the melting point of sand had a few admirers.

Dad whistled. 'You did a good job, kiddo. This display looks great.' He patted me on the back. 'Here, I'll go check your coat.'

Linda caught my eye from across the room and waved me over. I weaved my way through the crowd, past the case with the fake Midnight Star and a table groaning under the weight of too many hors d'oeuvres.

'Oh, Alice, isn't it wonderful. Everyone loves the display. And we're going to have a silent auction during intermission.'

'So the Beryl is going to be OK?' I asked. I didn't know how much money Irinke had donated, but Linda seemed a less worried than last night.

'Better than OK.' She looked around. 'Your father has been doing some digging at City Hall. I don't know what he found, but Rex Cragthorne seems terrified. He sent us all this champagne and has given us a very generous donation.' She smiled like a cat, practically licking the cream from her lips, and then sighed happily. 'He seems to have gotten the impression that if he stops trying to destroy the Beryl, I'll ask your father to stop digging.'

He must have gotten that impression from Linda. Once my dad was on the trail of a good story, nothing could shake him loose.

Linda smiled wickedly. 'Of course, he did try to destroy us, so I'm not sure if champagne and a donation is really enough, but we'll see.'

She gave me a smile so toothy, sharks would be jealous. I had a feeling Rex Cragthorne was going to be spending a lot of time with his lawyers in the near future. Then Linda spotted another potential donor and excused herself.

I made my way around the lobby to the large hors d'oeuvres table, ducking elbows and dodging small plates full of food, and started filling a plate of my own.

'Hey, Numbers.'

I looked around sharply. Kevin Jordan stood next to the table with his back against the wall. He wore a suit that showed a little too much of his socks and a striped green tie.

'Where have you been?' He looked at me and I could almost feel his relief. 'This kid is like superglue.'

I looked at the girl in the rainbow tutu. She had short dark hair and startlingly grey eyes.

'Benji?' I asked.

'It's short for Benjemima, apparently,' Kevin whispered.

I just stared.

'You thought I was a boy too, huh?' She smiled at me,

cheeks chipmunked with hors d'oeuvres.

My face grew hot. I knew better than to make assumptions. That was Detection 101.

Benji grabbed a handful of cheese puffs, and stuffed them into the pocket of her coat. 'It's cool,' she said, spitting crumbs. 'Why do you think the cops never catch me?'

The lights in the lobby blinked on and off, the signal that the show was about to start, and the murmur of casual conversation dimmed as we shuffled to our seats.

It was a full house. The air buzzed with excitement. I guess the thrill of seeing a show where the Phantom was caught trumped any safety concerns Rex Cragthorne might have managed to stir up. The lights dimmed all the way and the curtain rose.

I did my best to pay attention, but I couldn't stop thinking about the Midnight Star. Matthew Strange strode about the stage, delivering his lines and holding the audience in the palm of his hands. Kevin and Benji both sat still and glassy-eyed beside me. I think I actually heard people swooning. But every time the prop Midnight Star flashed onstage, I couldn't help wondering what had really happened all those years ago? *Where was the real Midnight Star now?*

At the end of Act One, Vivian tucked 'the Midnight Star' into the safe on the upper level of the set and then climbed into the bed, pretending to go to sleep. The lights dimmed and the scene changed. I sat up in my seat. I'd never watched the scene change before. I'd been too busy doing odd jobs.

The top level of the set – with Vivian still on it, in the bed – lifted into the fly space and the ground level spun slowly round to reveal an outdoor scene for a short piece between Della and Matthew, but I wasn't paying attention to the play now. I was wondering if Vivian Rollins was stuck up there on the set until it was lowered again at the beginning of the next Act. Stuck with the Midnight Star. And I wondered if Kittie Grace had been stuck that way too.

And with that factor added to the equation, it finally started to make sense. I sat through Act Two with a sense of impatience – not even watching properly while Della did her bit with opening the safe and taking out the Star. Or taking in how beautifully Mom had managed to rework the blue ballgown for Vivian. As soon as it ended, I was on my feet before the curtain touched the stage.

'Numbers?' Kevin asked.

I looked around desperately. 'I need to get backstage.'

I pushed my way into the aisle, ducking and weaving through the crowd like a salmon swimming upstream. The crowd thinned out as I got closer to the stage and I broke into a jog, ducked through the door at the foot of stage left and sprinted towards the dressing rooms.

'Where are we going?' Kevin said. He was close on my heels, jogging without any apparent effort. He grinned at me when he noticed how out of breath I was.

'I need to check something.'

I came around a corner and ran smack into Frank Vallance's broad chest. He took a step back and a deep breath in, raising one hand to his chest in dismay. Pete stood next to him, a script in one hand and a pencil in the other, making a series of notes.

'Sorry, Frank.' I doubled over and put my hands on my knees. I took a few more deep breaths, making sure my lungs were still working, then I turned to Pete. 'Pete, how accurate was your reconstruction of the set?'

'It was an exact replica. A lot of the parts are original.'

I nodded.

'So the safe in Vivian's bedroom. The only way to get to that would be from onstage?'

Pete nodded slowly.

'When it got lifted up for the set change, could someone standing on it reach the scaffolding beam next to the catwalk?'

Pete's eyes widened. His mouth fell open. He tried to speak, but he couldn't so he just nodded.

'And Frank, the script and the blocking. Is that true to the original production too?'

'Well, I may have made a few changes, but yes, for the most part it's the same.'

'Thanks,' I said, and I turned up the corridor and ran.

I hurtled into the wings of the theatre. I could hear foot-steps behind me, and a voice over the PA system droned:

Fifteen minutes to places for Act Three. Fifteen minutes.

'What are you doing?' Kevin asked.

'Don't you get it? We know the necklace went into the safe and then got lifted into the rafters. And when the set came back down, the necklace was gone.' I paused to catch my breath. 'It *had* to be Kittie Grace who took the necklace.'

'So she stole it while it was up there. So what? We still don't know what she did with it.'

'*So* the police report said that the constable in the audience locked down the stage after Act Two. There wouldn't be time for her to hand the diamond to an accomplice – she couldn't even have gone to her dressing room. She had to have hidden it up there between the two Acts. And she had to hide the Star before coming down from the catwalk, or down from the set.'

'But she never got back up there again to fetch it because of the fire,' Kevin added excitedly.

'Exactly!' I said, then shuddered, remembering the fire report. Kittie Grace had tried to go back, but the fire must have killed her before she could get to the Star. 'That's why Irinke must have been drilling those holes. She was looking for a secret compartment somewhere up there.'

'But there wasn't one.'

'No, but there must have been other places up there where Kittie could have hidden the diamond.' I was half-way up the ladder into the catwalk. Kevin was behind me.

'So you think it's still here?'

I slowed down and almost missed a rung. My stomach lurched to one side and I swallowed hard. 'I don't know,' I said. 'But if Irinke had found it, she wouldn't have hung around and fallen for our trap. It might still be there. You heard Pete – a lot of the set is from the original production.'

I got to the top of the catwalk.

I stood in the centre of the metal walkway and closed my eyes, counting up in primes and trying to calm my thoughts. Whoever hid the necklace would have needed somewhere safe, but also somewhere it would be easy to come back and get it without anyone getting suspicious. I opened my eyes and turned in a slow circle.

Nothing. The catwalk was clean and clutter-free to keep it safe. But that also meant that there weren't many places to hide things. The metal rungs, the wooden beams. The only things that weren't made of something solid were the sandbags that hung down from the ceiling.

And then it hit me. The sandbags.

The only reason I could reach all of them now was because the upper level of the set had been raised into the flies. When this part of the set was lowered back down, the sandbags – as their counterweight – would rise up into the darkness above my head and be well out of reach.

They were the perfect place for Kittie Grace to hide the Star. There were always more sandbags than the crew needed to counterbalance the set, so that if one came loose by accident the set wouldn't crash on to the stage. She could have untied one, put the necklace inside and then tied it back up.

I wondered if a police constable would even think to search them.

'Quick,' I said. 'The sandbags!'

I pulled the closest sandbag out of the space above the stage and opened it carefully. Kevin watched me for a second and then ran to the other end of the catwalk to start searching the ones hanging there.

I reached my hand into the clean smooth sand and brought it out empty. 'It isn't here,' I said.

'Not here either.'

We kept searching. There were twenty sandbags hanging from the flies. The Midnight Star wasn't in any of them.

I watched as a few loose grains of sand fell down on the stage below me and felt disappointment swirling around my middle. I had been so sure. I sighed and dropped to my knees.

What was I thinking? Surely Irinke had looked in the sandbags already. There was no point in searching them again. I thought maybe she'd missed one, but . . . I stopped. My eyes went wide and the dry dusty air of the theatre made them sting, but I was too shocked to blink. There *was* one sandbag left.

I climbed back down the ladder. I didn't bother going through the wings – I just shot straight through the red velvet curtains and jumped off the edge of the stage. A few audience members had returned to their seats and looked shocked to see me rocketing up the aisle but I ignored them.

I made it to the top of the theatre and pushed my way into the lobby. Kevin was right behind me. Pete trailed after us too.

Linda stood on the stairs that led up into the balcony; she was making a small speech of thanks. The Beryl's remaining patrons gathered around her like a flock of exotic birds, all dressed in sequins and feathers, although none of them held a candle to Irinke. But I wasn't there to see the donors. I looked around the lobby display. There.

I ran to the small display case next to the bathroom and lifted the lid.

Linda's speech faltered. 'Alice? What are you doing?' she asked in a voice full of horror as I lifted the vitrified sand-bag out of the case and smashed it to the concrete floor.

CHAPTER

33

$S$and and glass sprayed everywhere, coating the concrete floor. The people in the lobby gasped and stepped back, horrified.

'Alice, have you lost your mind?' Linda screeched again.

'Stay back,' I said and crouched, carefully avoiding a large shard of glass. I ran my fingers delicately through the chunks of glass and unmelted sand.

I had a terrifying moment of doubt, that I'd just smashed part of the lobby display in front of all Linda's potential patrons for nothing. And then my fingers closed around something cool and smooth. I lifted it slowly, blowing away the bits of sand that clung to the joints of the silver and diamond chain. I blinked. The pictures I'd seen hadn't started to do the necklace justice. The five diamond-encrusted chains sparkled in the light of the lobby display. Red rubies glinted where the chains joined together. And the teardrop diamonds that ran along the bottom row jingled slightly as I lifted it out of the sand.

I held the large diamond pendant at the base of the necklace to my lips and felt the stone go hot almost at once. It was real.

'Uh, Numbers?' Kevin's elbow in my ribs brought me back into the room. I looked up. Everyone was staring at me. Even my mom.

'Yeah,' I said lamely, swallowing hard. Then I took a deep breath and held the Midnight Star up into the light. 'I found it.'

There was a moment of total silence and then the room broke into thunderous applause. I felt myself turning a shade of red you only see on tomatoes. Kevin nudged me again and I shrugged and did my best to look graceful as I took a bow.

By the time I stood back up, Linda was standing beside me. She must have levitated over the crowd to get there so fast. I handed her the necklace and she took it with shaking hands. 'Are you sure?' she asked.

'You'll want to get it tested, but it's been hidden in that sandbag since the night of the fire. I think it's probably the real thing.'

People were snapping photos like it was going out of style. I saw Dad in the corner handing out business cards to everyone he saw. It wasn't exactly breaking news, but the theft of the Midnight Star in 1927 was a crime story. And Dad wouldn't be Dad if he let a juicy story like that go to waste.

Mom appeared out of the crowd a moment later, Della at her side. I couldn't believe Della was letting people see her during the interval, but I guess finding the Midnight Star was important enough that she could break the rules.

'You did it, honey,' Mom cried. 'I can't believe it.'

'I told you she was good at investigating,' Della said with a satisfied smile.

Kevin nodded his agreement, smiling so wide I could see his molars. Mom gave us each a stern look, but there wasn't much force behind it.

'I didn't get a chance to say thank you for my outfit,' I said. 'I really like it.'

Mom beamed, and smoothed the lapel of my jacket. 'I thought it would suit you.'

The warm glow from earlier burnt a little brighter. Maybe Mom understood me more than I thought.

The lobby lights flashed on and off. Intermission was over. Della gave a startled squeak and bolted through the doors, racing to get backstage before the curtain rose. After all, be it calamity or a miracle, the show must always go on. The lights flashed again, and Mom, Kevin and I went to find our seats to see the rest of the show.

*

Save the Beryl auctioned off the Midnight Star in early spring. It took a while to figure out who the necklace officially belonged to. In the end, a judge decided that, because Franklin Oswald had paid the original owner after the Star originally went missing, it belonged to the Beryl.

The necklace sold to an anonymous buyer in India. For twenty-five million dollars. More than enough to finish the Beryl's restoration and set up a trust for its care. There was even enough left over to start a free after-school programme to teach the next generation of theatre kids the tricks of the trade.

Benji was the first student to apply. She said she was passionate about learning special effects. I was pretty sure she just wanted to get her hands on some flash powder. But Pete seemed to have her under control.

'I still think we should have gotten a reward or something,' Kevin said, when he heard the news. 'After all we found it. *And* we caught the Phantom. We're heroes.'

'We?' I looked at him over the top of *Fermat's Last Theorem*. We were sitting in my living room waiting for the *Larry Sellers Show* to come on.

'Hey, I was there.'

I smirked. 'Linda offered to give us free tickets for life.'

Kevin didn't look impressed. He flopped back on the couch and sighed. Outside cold heavy rain drummed against the windows – winter was hanging on for dear life.

I shivered and snuggled further into the couch.

The theme music for the *Larry Sellers Show* started and Kevin shot to the edge of his seat.

Matthew Strange walked onstage. It was weird to see him on the TV after spending time with him in person. He flashed his trademark white smile and the audience practically swooned; so did Kevin. I smirked when I saw the bottle of apple water waiting next to his seat. Something told me the star was happy to be back in Hollywood.

'I can't believe you thought *he* might have been the bad guy,' Kevin scoffed without taking his eyes off the screen.

'I never said I thought it was him, I just said I couldn't rule him out just because he was famous.'

Kevin wasn't listening.

I sighed and went back to my book.

When the show was over, Kevin turned off the TV with a happy sigh. 'I still can't believe I got to meet him. In person.'

I grunted.

'And we solved another case. And caught an international jewel thief who Interpol has been chasing for years.'

Kevin paused. I could feel him building up to something.

'There's just one thing I'm disappointed about,' he said.

I turned the page and kept reading. I could feel Kevin's eyes on me, waiting for me to look up. I read two more pages and then put the book down.

'What are you disappointed about?' I asked.

Kevin's grin broadened. 'I would have really liked to see a ghost.' He wiggled his eyebrows at me and I shook my head with a laugh.

In a minute, Dad would come back with takeaway from the Vietnamese place up the street and the smell of chilli and lime would fill the house, we'd eat and Dad would tell us the latest developments in the case against Rex Cragthorne.

But right now I was warm and comfortable and I had a chapter to finish.

x plus y plus z equalled perfect.

ACKNOWLEDGEMENTS

This is my third book, but my first sequel, and I leant on a lot of people as I undertook this new challenge. To everyone who listened to me worry and fret about getting it right, thank you!

In particular, I'd like to thank my agent, Lindsey Fraser, for her constant support and for helping me find the way to start. Thanks also to the amazing editor chickens Rachel Leyshon and Kesia Lupo for helping me take a lot of events and distil them into an exciting and coherent plot.

I'd also like to thank my wonderful writing group, the KiDS (Dave, Celeste, Noel, Kim, Ariel and Geoff) for reading some very messy early drafts and helping me save the good bits and get rid of the bad and reminding me when my characters disappeared from a scene.

Thank you to my husband, Chris, for listening to me try to untangle plot snarls, being my maths consultant, and bringing me tea and ice cream; to my son Henry for reminding me of the magic of reading; and a very, very special thank you to my daughter Matilda, for waiting to be born until after I finished the first draft!

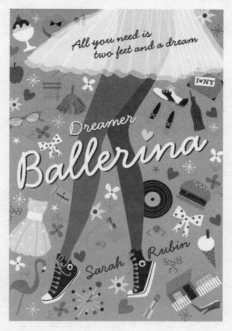

DREAMER BALLERINA by SARAH RUBIN

All you need is a dream and two feet!
Casey Quinn has got to dance. It's in her bones.

She's got more grace in her pinkie toe than all those prissy ballet-school girls put together, though you'd never guess it from her skinny white chicken-legs and her hand-me-down ballet shoes.

When Casey shuts her eyes, she sees the bright lights of the New York City stage.

She's going to get there. Somehow.

'Deftly balancing themes of good fortune and passion, hope and heartache, Rubin's fine debut will appeal widely to artists and dreamers alike.'
PUBLISHERS WEEKLY

Paperback, ISBN 978-1-906427-61-0, £6.99

BEETLE BOY by M. G. LEONARD

Darkus can't believe his eyes when a huge insect drops out of the trouser leg of his horrible new neighbour. It's a giant beetle – and it seems to want to communicate.

But how can a boy be friends with a beetle? And what does a beetle have to do with the disappearance of his dad and the arrival of Lucretia Cutter, with her taste for creepy jewellery?

'A darkly funny Dahl-esque adventure.'
KATHERINE WOODFINE, AUTHOR

Paperback, ISBN 978-1-910002-70-4, £6.99 • ebook, ISBN 978-1-910002-98-8, £6.99

THE MYSTERIOUS BENEDICT SOCIETY

by TRENTON LEE STEWART

When a peculiar advertisement appears in the newspaper for children to take part in a secret mission, children everywhere sit a series of mysterious tests. In the end, just Reynie, Kate, Sticky and Constance succeed. They have three things in common: they are honest, remarkably talented and orphans.

They must go undercover at the Learning Institute for the Very Enlightened. There they must work as a team to save not only themselves, but also the world outside the walls.

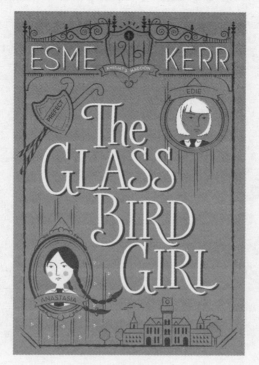

THE GLASS BIRD GIRL by ESME KERR

Edie is sent to Knight's Haddon to keep an eye on Anastasia, the daughter of a wealthy Russian prince. But what she discovers at the castle-like boarding school is that nobody is quite as they seem. And when a precious glass bird goes missing, only Edie sees the bigger mystery unfolding . . .

'. . . perfect for Blyton fans — and girls dreaming of adventure.'
MAIL ON SUNDAY

'. . . it really hits the spot.'
BOOKS FOR KEEPS

Paperback, ISBN 978-1-910002-67-4, £6.99 • ebook, ISBN 978-1-909489-55-4, £6.99

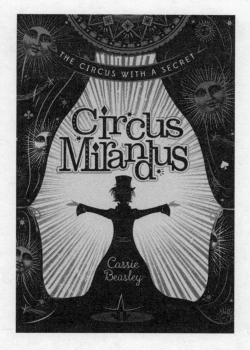

CIRCUS MIRANDUS by CASSIE BEASLEY

Micah's beloved grandfather is sick, but all is not lost. Years ago, he visited a mysterious circus where he was promised a miracle by a man who could bend light.

But who is this stranger, and will he keep his word? Micah sets out to find the magical Circus Mirandus, but does it really exist?

'Heart-warming and charming . . . if you love Roald Dahl it's definitely worth a read.'
EVENING GAZETTE

Paperback, ISBN 978-1-910002-57-5, £6.99 • ebook, ISBN 978-1-910002-58-2, £6.99